The Bubble Star

The Bubble Star

•

Lesley-Anne Bourne

The Porcupine's Quill

CANADIAN CATALOGUING IN PUBLICATION DATA

Bourne, Lesley-Anne, 1964–
The bubble star

ISBN 0-88984-199-3

I. Title.

PS8553.0856B82 1998   C813'.54   C98-931919-9
PR9199.3.B68B82 1998

Published by The Porcupine's Quill,
68 Main Street, Erin, Ontario NOB ITO.
Readied for the press by John Metcalf; copy edited by Doris Cowan.
Typeset in Galliard, printed on Zephyr Antique laid,
and bound at The Porcupine's Quill Inc.

The cover image, *Never Mind* (mixed media on paper, 70.5x48 cm., 1997),
is reproduced with the kind permission of Kelley Aitken.

Represented in Canada by the Literary Press Group.
Trade orders are available from General Distribution Services.

We acknowledge the support of the Ontario Arts Council,
and the Canada Council for the Arts for our publishing program.
The financial support of the Government of Canada
through the Book Publishing Industry Development Program
is also gratefully acknowledged.

I 2 3 4 • OO 99 98

Acknowledgements

•

For reading the manuscript in its various stages yet still encouraging me, my gratitude goes to the following: Anne-Louise Brookes, Irene Guilford, Deirdre Kessler, Laura Lush, Jay Ruzesky, and Jane Urquhart. For wisdom and endurance through the final stages, thank you to John Metcalf.

For their helpfulness and kind support, many thanks go to the following: Cantaloupe, Donna, Kelley Aitken, Dr Padraig Darby, Nigel Guilford, Stephen B. MacInnis, Larry Yeo, the writers and facilitators at the Banff Centre in October 1995, the PEI Council for the Arts, the Canada Council, and the Bank of Mom and Dad.

The chapter 'Junction' appeared in a shorter version in *eye wuz here – stories by women writers under 30* (Douglas & McIntyre), edited by Shannon Cooley, who started the ball rolling.

Lastly, for seeing it all, love & thanks to my husband, Richard Lemm.

•

When you were six you thought mistress meant to put your shoes on the wrong feet.

— Lorrie Moore, *How to Be an Other Woman*

Her heart has a rule of thumb for the few people she does meet: if the dark figure comes toward her at a walk her heart goes on alert and her arm presses her shoulder bag tight to her side, but if the figure comes at her in a run her heart and arm don't respond at all. All the thief would have to do, she thinks, is jog.

— Elisabeth Harvor, *Heart Trouble*

Junction

•

Her whole life Imogene had loved Benny. She thought about this while lying next to him in the bed he shared with his wife. Martha was at Goodmart where she worked as a cashier.

An *express* cashier, she'd correct people when they described her position.

She wouldn't be home until four.

* * *

Benny had only recently come back into Imogene's life. She'd had car trouble, specifically, her car was billowing white smoke one afternoon during rush hour, well, what was considered to be rush hour in a place like Willow Junction. And what kind of a name was Willow Junction? she thought as it passed her as a bus destination. Once when the bus roared towards her, the first three letters had disappeared or burned out or fallen back behind where the destination or route was supposed to be spelled out. The junction sounded even worse then, if that was possible. The sad thing was, it perfectly described the area she was born in and which she'd never left.

Rush hour meant about twenty more cars than usual passed through the main highway intersection. This happened at precisely five-ten. Ten minutes allowing for the drive from town, from the city, Bay Lake. And, thought Imogene, that was another dumb name! Was it a bay? Or a lake? Couldn't the city also be called Lake Bay? Leave it to city folk to screw up like that, she reasoned when she was a kid, they couldn't make up their minds.

Imogene figured her car was about number twelve through the intersection. Or it would have been, that Tuesday, when the car started smoking. Then it died. Cars angrily swerved around her as if she'd planned the scene, as if she'd always wanted that kind of power and had worked and worked to develop the moment. She rested her head on the wheel. Sun burned her left arm. Her hair completely hid her face and she thought, I'm not Imogene, I'm Imagine.

She'd done this since she was a kid. Since her mother had told her one day that they named her after the actress, Imogene Coca. An actress, said her mother, is a film star. Someone who pretends to be someone else, and gets paid for it.

Imagine, her mother said that afternoon long ago when Imogene was crying, you are some place you really want to be, and you are doing something you really want to do.

She said this because Imogene was crying, actually wailing, by the side of the sink. She was standing above the sink, on the bathroom counter, naked. Her mother had been washing Imogene's feet or something, and had lifted her daughter from the soapy water. As always, her mother had gently lifted the girl with, Imogene considered, the hands of a swan. Or, more precisely, she corrected her imagination, the wings of a swan. She'd just recently seen the white birds while on a car trip with her cousins. They'd all driven five hours south to a theatre town. Culture, her mother had said as they ate Cheezies in the backseat on the long hot drive there. Imogene thought her mother said vulture, and from then on the drive seemed to be headed straight into dread. So when the vultures turned out to be swans, Imogene was more than relieved. Still, she didn't venture that close to the birds floating in the river or standing on the grass. Melanie, a city cousin, went right up to one, her fat hands out to pet it, of course.

Melanie's mother had screamed first, just before Melanie. Sure enough, the bird grabbed on for a second. From then on, Imogene thought of her cousin as Meal. Instead of Mel, as the little girl wanted to be called, having had a novel read to her with a character named Little Nell in it, Imogene would say, Meal.

Imogene's mother's belt buckle had scratched her daughter's stomach. I hate these bell-bottoms anyway and who the hell needs hip-huggers, she said through tears, and what if the buckle's rusty?

Imogene didn't understand, and stopped sobbing to listen. That was when her mother had told her about the name.

Imagine, Imogene told herself in the hot Mustang, you are on a beach, Silver Beach say, behind the Bamboo Garden, with Benny. Okay, she thought as someone honked behind her, that takes care of the where. Now what am I doing that I want to do?

She pictured Benny, his round tanned face, the cluster of red bumps that seemed always to circle his chin. She thought they were like the strawberry patch they'd stretched out in that time he'd asked to see what was under her T-shirt.

Nothing is under my T-shirt, she said, not getting it.

But Benny, a year older, had persevered and they had seen each other without clothes on. The strawberries had squished in places and so they wrote their names on each other with the juice. Benny had written his right across her chest. An 'n' landed on each developing breast. There was a nice balance to that, she thought, scrunching her chin to look down.

She wasn't nearly so bold and wrote 'Imogene' on his stomach. As she was writing it, in penmanship far better than anything she'd ever written for Miss Reynolds, she did manage to glance further south. She'd never seen anything like it.

Is it heavy? she wanted to know.

Okay, Silver Beach behind the Bamboo Gardens with Benny.

It sounded to her a lot like when she'd played that game, what was it, Clue? Probably with Benny. Silver Beach behind the Bamboo Gardens with Benny and ...

And? Didn't the game say there had to be a weapon?

And a rope.

The rope had been around Benny's dog's neck. The dog was named God. Benny had named the dog and thought himself the only one to reverse letters ever. It was a good name, thought Imogene, especially on Sundays when the dog went missing. She and Benny would wander the woods and the field next to the church. The sign, for as long as Imogene could remember, had said Ye Must Be Born Again. This, at the corner into Willow Junction. Did this mean, she had often wondered, growing up, that every time her father, Ray, drove to work, and every time he came home, that he had to imagine his birth all over again? That was twice a day, almost three hundred and sixty-five days a year, because he hardly ever missed work. And, what if someone couldn't remember their birth?

Imogene couldn't remember hers, though she'd been told often enough that she was fast and that she'd tried, in her hurry, to come out left leg and right arm first. The doctor used to like to tell her every time she went for a check-up that he'd had to reach in and turn her around. He said it was like trying to get a pop out of one of those new machines. If it wasn't turned the right way, like on its side, you couldn't get the can out. Imogene couldn't quite follow what he was talking about, and couldn't connect why her mother turned red each time Dr Wilson said these things, but she smiled at the man anyway.

God would go missing while church was in. Sunday evening, the two of them would be in the woods, calling for God. Inevitably, a kid would get up from where he sat in the pews and would look out the window. Was this part of the service? Could they all go outside to look for God?

Late at night, Imogene would hear Benny's voice calling God.

I'm on a beach. We're walking God, and Benny is kissing me.

Someone knocked on her head.

Oh, sorry, I thought your window was up.

It was Benny beside the Mustang.

If you steer, I can push you into the station.

Sure enough, there was the blue and red gas station right beside the car. But where had Benny come from?

Did I imagine him?

Imogene was asking herself all these things and was trying to steer and to fix her face in the rear view mirror. Instead, she just kept seeing the brown torso of Benny. His open flannel shirt was brown too, plaid. And it was stained with grease.

She looked at her watch: five-twenty.

I was just leaving, said Benny, when I saw the line of cars. And the steam. It's probably your rad.

It was as if they'd never stopped talking. As if they'd seen each other every day. As if neither had ever married.

* * *

There were no willows in Willow Junction. Lots of poplar, pine, and spruce. Some maple. But no willows. The first one Imogene saw was in her aunt and uncle's backyard one Christmas. Imogene, her sisters, Janis and Peggy-Leigh, and her parents drove to Toronto for the holiday. They drove their new blue station wagon. A Chrysler, she remembered from staring at the dash from the very back all that time. She had no idea what a Chrysler was, but it felt good in the mouth when she said it. Chrysler, she went around saying the night they got it.

It was after ballet class. Ballet was her mother's idea. Imogene didn't mind, she liked to swing from the barre like an ape. After class, when she walked out to the car, her father wasn't the only one picking her up. The whole family was there.

What's going on? Imogene asked as she climbed into the front seat, crawled over her mother and flipped into the back seat on top of Janis and Peggy-Leigh. The back doors hadn't opened for months. Peggy-Leigh helped her over into the way-back as they called it, by pushing her bum hard and heaving her dance bag on top of her.

A surprise, said her father. He tossed his cigarette into the winter night. It was only half smoked, which made Imogene wonder what could be so special.

The car lot lights made the cars look like liquid. Shiny blots of Kool-aid. She liked the red ones best. She counted them as her father sat at a desk inside with a man in a purple blazer. Her mother didn't say anything, she just looked out the passenger-side window, longingly, at the trucks, thought Imogene.

And then they went to A&W. In the new blue station wagon. The way-back had plush blue carpet which her father didn't want to get dirty. He said, So don't spill your root beer. They sat in front of the drive-in with all the windows down, even the one in the back. Her father had put that one down for Imogene. They'd never had electric ones before.

They waited. The waitresses in their orange-and-brown short dresses chatted happily inside near the counter.

Should we go in, Ray?

It's a drive-in, Iris.

But they're not coming out, honey. Maybe we should go in?

Peggy-Leigh tossed Imogene's dance bag back. It had only made it as far as the backseat during the transfer. They'd all been a bit distracted by the free trip to Florida. It turned out that anyone buying a new Chrysler in December, the week before Christmas, got a free trip to Florida in March. Imogene's father said he hadn't known and wasn't that a special surprise. Her mother simply stared with part of her lip gone into her mouth.

So the five had dashed into the new car all talking about Florida. Somehow Imogene ended up in the way-back, though she'd been hoping for the backseat. She had thought it best to try to stake out her territory right from the beginning. But apparently her older sister, Peggy-Leigh, and her younger sister, Janis, had the same idea.

Honey?

What?

Let's go in, maybe it's too cold for the waitresses to come out.

It's a drive-in for chrissakes, that's the point, Iris.

Imogene tried to cheer them up. Will they have A&Ws in Florida? Her father laughed and opened his door. Ah, a sign, she thought and plopped down on top of Peggy-Leigh.

Hey, get off me!

And then they were inside ordering Baby Burgers, a Teen Burger, a Momma Burger, and two Papa Burgers. The best part, they all agreed, was the ice on the mugs. Imogene could hardly lift hers but that didn't matter. They loved A&W. In summer they'd come with Imogene's grandfather in his Volkswagen.

Imogene's mother even let them order onion rings. It was a special night, they all agreed.

The first thing Imogene noticed about her aunt and uncle's place in Toronto was a tree. Sticking out of the patchy snow, it was a long and twisted thing, skinny, almost artificial, she decided. There were long ropes where branches should have been. And the trunk was a trail to be followed. Imogene and her sisters rolled out of the station wagon and immediately climbed the tree. When Aunt Ed walked out, the girls squawked, pretending to be exotic birds.

Their snowsuits were intentionally different colours so that their mother could readily tell them apart. It was the same principle, she explained to the girls, as having a black kitten instead of a white one. When they'd picked Woodstock the year before, they'd gone for the dark one because their mother said they'd step on one that matched their kitchen floor. This had made all three girls burst into tears. First Janis. And then Imogene, who was a sympathetic cryer. She cried whenever anyone else did, the same way she threw up when her father had come home in the middle of the night from a golf tournament sponsored by the local brewery. Peggy-Leigh started to cry because, she said, her sisters were so stupid and were taking so long and why couldn't she have her own kitten, after all, she was old enough to take care of it and she wouldn't be dumb enough to squash its guts out. The other two girls wailed at this and their mother apologized to the owner of the kittens and said they all needed a nap.

Peggy-Leigh's suit was bright green. Janis had a pink and orange one. Imogene's was yellow. She hated yellow, and imagined her suit was red.

The girls stayed in the tree a long time, swaying the rope branches back and forth the same way they played with the skin under their aunt's arms. That was the last time she'd visited. Their mother warned them this time not to do that as Aunt Ed didn't seem to like it. Why wouldn't she, thought Imogene, wouldn't it feel good?

The next morning was Christmas. The girls had just dumped out their stockings, when there was a knock at the front door. Uncle Keith answered it. A big policeman wanted to know who the blue station wagon belonged to.

Imogene threw up. She had eaten too much chocolate too fast, and had eaten half of the red jelly beans before drinking two glasses of orange juice. And she was scared. As her mother led her to the kitchen to clean her up, Imogene cried, What's wrong? Is Daddy going to jail?

It turned out that someone had hit the back of the car. It had been parked behind the house, in an alley. The officer figured it had happened in the middle of the night.

* * *

There was an afternoon once, after Imogene's mother's operation, when just she and her mother were home. Imogene wasn't sure what kind of operation it had been, just that it was serious, and that it had been somewhere near the stomach. And her mother was tired and weak and wasn't to be disturbed.

Imogene was playing with Barbie. She hated Barbie. She'd only insisted on having the doll because Peggy-Leigh had a zillion of them and was always playing with their beach buggies and campers and houses with pools. Imogene had ripped Barbie's arm off almost as soon as she got the doll.

Well, she said, I couldn't get her dress on. It was too tight, her arm wouldn't fit in, so I took it off to put the sleeve on and then it wouldn't stay put.

She demonstrated as her mother looked on. The arm slid out of the pink sequined sleeve and plunked onto the floor. It lay there, palm up, as if waiting for someone to hold its hand and to lead it somewhere. Imogene's mother shuddered, which surprised Imogene because it was summer.

It was summer and she was stuck indoors with one-armed Barbie. She wanted to be outside, sitting in her father's red Mustang.

The car was kept locked, under a tarp, and was parked on blocks in the backyard. But Imogene knew the key was on a nail inside the Tupperware cupboard. She had a habit of sneaking under the tarp, sitting behind the wheel, and imagining she was a famous race car driver. Or, at the very least, that she was a regular grown-up person driving away from Willow Junction. Or, that she was her father. Why had he wanted to buy this car, just to put it in the backyard? When Imogene asked her father this he said something about her sounding just like her mother and something else about wanting to hang onto something. Her father mumbled and seemed to be looking toward the highway. Imogene's mother called it his bachelor car. What's a bachelor? Imogene asked.

Imogene was supposed to stay in the house in case her mother needed anything. But she wasn't supposed to bug her mother, she needed rest.

Imogene?

She let Barbie crash to the floor as she got up. Why they couldn't make the doll so that she could stand up, Imogene didn't know. The feet were on tiptoe. Who walks like that? she wondered, but did like the way the feet were easy to get into the tiny pink plastic high heels.

Mom?

There was no response. Imogene left her room and walked down the hallway.

Did you want something, Mom?

Still, there was no answer, so Imogene poked her head around her parents' bedroom door.

Her eyes always went to one spot first. The brown design on the blue wall. Imogene hoped it was gone, but it was still there. Like a secret message, or a painting in caves like she'd seen in cartoons, it waited. She'd put it there. By accident.

Peggy-Leigh had discovered painting-by-numbers. This one was of a horse. Imogene hated horses. She didn't see the point and couldn't understand why all kinds of girls in her class collected horses. They had ceramic ones, plastic ones, and stuffed ones. Stupid horses, thought Imogene. But the painting wasn't bad, as far as horses went. And Peggy-Leigh stayed in all the lines, it was good, said Imogene.

She'd just wanted to know if it was dry. But Imogene knew not to touch it. Peggy-Leigh had expressly said, Don't touch it. It's not dry, and I don't want you smearing it.

And then Peggy-Leigh put the work of art in their parents' bedroom which was off-limits.

So, very carefully, Imogene picked it up by the edges. She looked. She looked closer. It looked dry. It smelled dry. She tilted it. No paint ran. As one final check, Imogene put it flat against the blue bedroom wall, and pressed it.

When she pulled the painting back, there were little brown marks, almost in the shape of the horse's face.

Imogene thought her life was over. She had trouble breathing. She managed to look at the painting. It hadn't smeared. She must have put it straight against the wall and then pulled it straight back, no movement side to side. But the wall clearly had paint on it. She moved the big upholstered chair in front. The brown could hardly be seen.

She got caught. Peggy-Leigh screamed that she'd ruined the painting. Her parents yelled that she'd ruined the wall.

And there it was, still there, like a hole in a tree.

Mom?

Her mother said something. Imogene moved closer to the bed. Her mother looked awful. White with sweat running down her face and she said she was freezing. Imogene was scared.

Are you okay?

I think you'd better go across the street and get Mrs Johnson.

Really?

Imogene didn't want to. She had this thing about going over to the Johnsons. Ever since Willy had told her to come in, go upstairs, my Mom wants to talk to you.

To me? Why?

I don't know, she just said for you to go upstairs, that she had something to tell you, Willy said, his sneakers kicking the open front door.

So Imogene went up. Slowly up the green carpeted stairs. She turned the corner and called, Mrs Johnson?

There was no answer.

She stood in the upstairs hallway, wondering which room Mrs Johnson was in.

Mrs Johnson?

She heard Mrs Johnson say something, but she couldn't make it out. She followed the voice to the end of the hall. Why didn't Willy tell me which room? And why didn't he come up with me?

She was thinking too late and she knew it.

Later, she wasn't sure if she'd heard Willy's laughter before or after.

Before or after she saw Mrs Johnson naked, lying on the bed and talking on the telephone.

Get Mrs Johnson, Imogene's mother had said, I think I'm bleeding.

Imogene had run across the lawn thinking, Where is the blood?

That was one of the times she'd been credited with saving her parents' lives. Apparently some folks could be allergic to anaesthetic, said Dr Marson, the specialist. And Imogene's mother was. She hadn't been bleeding, that was just one of the many sensations. She'd had dangerously low blood pressure, and other reactions, and when Dr Marson arrived, having been called by a clothed Mrs Johnson, he said it had been just in time.

For what? Imogene asked from the doorway to her parents' room.

The doctor, Mrs Johnson, and her mother all stared at her, as if they'd never heard her speak before. Imogene had noticed adults did that once in a while, looked as if pig Latin had just been spoken. Peggy-Leigh could speak it with her friend Pam and Imogene had no idea what they were saying. She hated that.

* * *

I'm pregnant, said Imogene.

She'd hoped not to say it like that. She'd imagined a nice quiet dinner at the back of Rosetta's Restaurant. Some garlic bread, ravioli, maybe they could share a dessert.

But things hadn't worked out.

It was the wine. Benny wanted to order some red wine as soon as they had arrived. She said no to a bottle, perhaps he could just have some by the glass?

Bottle's cheaper, he said.

Not if I'm not drinking any, she said.

Since when have you turned down wine? he said winking at Imogene and then winking at the waitress in red gingham.

I'm pregnant, Imogene said.

The waitress looked up from her small yellow pad and click pen. She looked at Imogene, then at Benny. Then Imogene and Benny looked at her. She left.

What?

Pregnant, said Imogene, You know, with a baby?

Benny had this look. This look she couldn't read. His eyebrows went flat like the brim of the caps he wore which said John Deere or Evinrude.

He stretched his leg out, towards Imogene, and it hit her foot. She left her foot there, touching him. She needed some kind of contact.

Does it hurt? she asked.

She meant his leg, the one he'd injured.

No, he said.

But she knew he was lying. His leg often hurt. Ever since that accident with his dirt bike, he'd had pain. They said the bike hit something in the sand, tossed Benny, and then drove over him.

He'd been riding too fast on Silver Beach. When she was finally allowed to see him at St. Mary's, he was still covered in sand. When he nodded his head to say Yeah, I'm okay, sand rained down onto the hospital sheet. She could see it under his nails. The traction chains and bolts and handles glinted in the sun.

He spent that summer that way. And in the fall, they learned his leg was short. By a good inch. And he wasn't the kind to wear special shoes.

Okay, he said, so it hurts.

She wondered which he was talking about and hoped it was his leg.

I thought you were on the pill?

I am, she said, it happens.

* * *

She'd spent her first few years on the pill dreading that she might be the one it happened to. Peggy-Leigh had lots of magazines that said things like *You can still get pregnant no matter what you do.* Imogene snuck them from her older sister's room. She locked herself in the bathroom, sat on the floor, and read the magazine page by page, being careful not to crease anything or to leave finger grease on the cover. Her sister had caught her before. Not because she hadn't put the magazine back at exactly the right angle, with the right number of beads or hair ribbons arranged in their proper code, but because she'd marked the cover model's face with her finger grease. Finger grease was Peggy-Leigh's term. After that, Imogene would read a magazine almost without touching it. It was on the floor and Imogene, having washed and dried her hands, gently lifted the pages one by one by their bottom corner. She never again touched the cover.

Story after story told the horror of getting pregnant when you were fifteen. No time of the month was safe. Nothing worked one hundred percent. How can people publish stuff like this? she wanted to know.

* * *

Those antibiotics I was on for my ear infection? They must have wiped out my pill.

Imogene imagined the two drugs in her body. They were professional arm wrestlers. And during their struggle, one overpowered the other. The defender of the sperm, as she called it, won. The challenger, her birth control, succumbed.

Benny fiddled with the iceberg lettuce in front of him. The waitress apologized when she brought it, as if she was sorry to be there, but what could she do?

The baby wasn't the problem. Imogene had wanted a child for two years. The last twenty-four periods had her in tears every single time. Each red sign broke her heart. Again and again, she hoped her period would not come. But she couldn't go off the pill. Russ didn't think the time was right and she couldn't bear to resort to tricking him. She hoped that nature would somehow overtake technology.

And the problem wasn't that Imogene and Benny weren't married. They were. To other people.

* * *

Florida wasn't all it was cracked up to be. Then again, the brochure they'd found in the glove compartment of their new blue station wagon was hard to believe. The pool was empty, without a ripple, and was the colour of Windex. The palm trees ever so slightly leaned to one side as if a gentle breeze was just passing through mid-afternoon. The shot of the beach at night showed a path lit by little coloured lamps in the shapes of fruit. No one was around. Peace. One photo showed a family of five playing in the surf at sunset. Could life get any better?

But the drive down hadn't been much fun. They hit snow in three states. And then the car died in Georgia. On railroad tracks.

Imogene was about to throw up while the other four passengers yelled about what they should do, when a pick-up truck drove up beside them.

Need help?

By the question, Imogene wondered if maybe the people who lived in the town regularly got stuck on railway tracks.

Yep, said her father. Could you give us a push?

Two men stepped from the truck. While the doors were open, Imogene could hear strange sounds from inside.

What's that? She asked the man nearest her window.

My cock.

Her mother turned around. Imogene! Don't you bother the man, he's trying to help us. Let him concentrate now, your father is trying to get us off the tracks.

Cock fights, he said. You know, birds?

And then they were safe. Not far from the tracks, but far enough. They could see a gas station within walking distance.

By that night the car was running again. And the next day they would be in Florida. Imogene pulled the crumpled brochure out of her knapsack. Her sister turned around from the back seat and watched this. You make me sick, Peggy-Leigh said.

It turned out that Fort Lauderdale was a big place. Like Toronto, only hotter, and pastel-coloured. Imogene couldn't see where they'd taken the pictures from. The brochure showed a kidney-shaped pool. The one at the hotel was square. And cracked. And not the colour of Windex. And there were green things growing on the sides. Imogene's mother said, without getting out of the car, No one is swimming in that.

Ray, she called as his back disappeared into the door marked Office, ask for a quiet room.

The beach wasn't, as the brochure suggested, just beyond the sliding glass doors in each room. It was across the street. Across the six-lane street, and down a bit. Apparently you couldn't cut through another hotel's lobby, you had to walk until you reached a sign that said Public Access.

What's Public Access? Imogene asked her mother who was loaded down with a straw beach bag filled with towels, pails, four kinds of suntan lotion, pop, nose plugs, and a romance novel.

It means we shouldn't have bought the car.

Their first night in the Capri, Imogene awoke when her mother screamed. Imogene was on the couch. Peggy-Leigh and Janis shared one double bed, their parents the other.

What's wrong? said Ray.

A bug, said Iris. A big bug. Ray, kill it!

She was nearly hysterical, thought Imogene who wasn't used to her mother saying words like 'kill'. Her mother kept pointing and crying.

Ray!

Imogene's father got out of bed, walked over and stopped where his wife was pointing.

I don't see anything.

Well, look! It's huge and black and ugly and why the hell are we staying in this dump!

Imogene waited for her father's answer. Janis and Peggy-Leigh were pretending to sleep. Janis had pulled her pillow over her head and Imogene could see it shaking up and down.

Imogene imagined she was playing cards. With Benny. In a tent in the backyard. Benny and the Queen of Diamonds. She rolled over. She could hear her mother quietly crying into her father's undershirt. He must have put his arm around her.

Imogene was feeling sleepy again. Benny. And she was the queen. And there were diamonds everywhere inside the tent.

The next day their father told them they would only be staying one more night.

But that's only two nights, said Peggy-Leigh. We get three more free nights.

You get what you pay for, said Imogene's mother to no one.

Never mind, said her father, we're going to find somewhere else.

I don't see why we can't just go now, said her mother.

Because, Iris, we're booked for the free tour at ten.

The free tour was billed as a great family breakfast, a visit to an orange grove, and a visit to the Everglades. It was scheduled from ten until five. They climbed into the van.

Imogene noticed there were no other kids. There were only three couples who all had white hair. The van pulled onto the road.

This isn't so bad, said Imogene's father as they climbed back into the van after walking through the orange trees. Imogene had seen her parents holding hands as they ducked blossoms and oranges. Oranges that weren't really orange, they were green. Why are they called oranges if they're green? she asked her parents. Peggy-Leigh elbowed her as they walked behind their guide.

Back in the van, the guide used his hand-held walkie-talkie again to tell them to their right was the Everglades. Imogene couldn't see anything except a swamp. A boring green swamp. Where? she asked. The guide must not have heard her.

We won't be stopping, he continued on, it's much too dangerous. You know, snakes and alligators. Or is it crocodiles? Well, he laughed, they can both eat you.

Not stopping! said Imogene. She was devastated. She looked at her watch, was it near five already? It seemed to her like they'd just had breakfast at a restaurant called Denny's, which reminded her of Benny, so she bought him a postcard there, and then had that quick tour of the orange grove. It couldn't be that late.

It was noon. Just then, the van turned in through some fancy gates. The sign said Seaside Acres.

We have a surprise for you, said the guide happily.

Imogene's mother looked at the guide.

It's okay, said Imogene's father, it's probably lunch.

We're offering you a free lunch.

There's no free lunch, said Imogene's mother to Imogene.

Yes, there is, Mom, he just said so.

Lunch was macaroni and cheese with too much pepper. The girls didn't eat a lot. And then a smiling blond woman appeared and said they were to go with her to the pool.

But we don't have our swimsuits, said Imogene.

The woman smiled a little less. Well, you can look at the pool, can't you?

She put her arm around Imogene and pushed her. Janis looked back at their father.

It's okay, he smiled. Have a good time.

Imogene wasn't so easily convinced. She walked back to her mother. I want to stay. Why would I want to see a pool I can't swim in?

Peggy-Leigh and Janis had already disappeared with the blond woman.

Okay, sweetie, her mother sighed, Whatever you want. We should be going soon anyway, she said, looking at her husband.

Hi.

A big man was shaking Imogene's father's hand. I'm Jim. James really, but we're not formal here, we're more like family in this community, so call me Jim.

He offered his hand to Imogene's mother. She looked at it. Then she looked at her husband.

He shrugged and shook his head slightly.

Who are you? Imogene asked.

I'm Jim, he smiled, I just told your parents that.

No, I mean, who are you? Imogene said, dropping her knapsack in frustration.

Oh, well, I work here. I'm a real estate agent, he smiled. Do you know what a real estate agent is? he asked Imogene.

I do, said her mother.

Now, honey, said Imogene's father, give him a chance.

Where's our guide? I want to go now, Imogene said.

Well, sweetie, we have a lovely pool outside.

She's staying with us, said Imogene's mother.

And your name is?

Iris.

Well, Iris and, ah, your name sir?

His name is Charles, said Iris.

Imogene looked.

Charles Fountaine, the Third, said Imogene's mother while looking directly at the garden fountain through the window.

Oh, said Jim. Well let's get started, shall we?

Seaside Acres, it turned out, was a recent development. The perfect life. A quiet subdivision right on its own golf course. There were pathways everywhere for golf carts.

Great, said Imogene, does everyone get to drive one?

Jim was showing pictures and plans to Imogene's parents. They'd been in his office for close to two hours. They saw slides and books, and heard how there were only a few properties left so they should hurry.

Well, began Imogene's father, We're really not sure . . .

Charles means, interrupted Imogene's mother, we're really not sure we want something this small. We were hoping for something really grand.

Jim smiled at her.

Imogene's mother continued, After all, Charles, she said putting her hand on his sunburned arm, we already have the chalet. It's fine but rather small and really, if we have a ski place, we should have a warm place to golf as well.

Imogene's father looked lost.

Jim looked like he would burst and he handed another plan to Imogene's mother.

Iris, he said, then this is for you. I was saving this.

Imogene's mother unrolled the big paper. Lines went everywhere.

It's three stories, gushed Jim. The rest are only bungalows. And this is right near the eighteenth. It's luxury at its best.

Is there a playground? asked Imogene.

No, dear, said Jim. There aren't really any kids here. This is a place, he smiled, for adults.

Imogene looked to her mother. Her mother winked at her.

Oh, that's fine. They're away at private school most of the time, anyway.

Why was her mother lying Imogene wondered. Her father looked miserable.

I think you should draw it up.

Right away, said Jim.

Now, just a minute, honey, said Imogene's father, you can't . . .

I know, said her mother, we can't buy one without your sister buying one too, but we'll just have to tell her to call Seaside Acres right away.

Imogene knew her father didn't have a sister. She looked at Jim. Jim found all the proper papers and wrote in the proper conditions while Imogene and her parents sat in the hot little office watching. Iris led Jim on while Imogene's father sat silent.

With pen poised over paper, Imogene's mother looked up and looked Jim straight in the eye.

Jim, she said, I hate Seaside Acres.

Imogene and her father stared open-mouthed.

There's no sea. The houses are ugly. Golf is a stupid game. And we'd never be part of a place that doesn't like kids. You've got a lot of nerve leading tourists into a trap like this and you can bet the Better Business Bureau will be hearing from us. And, she said, handing the pen back to Jim, you can kiss your commission goodbye.

* * *

Benny poured himself more wine even though almost none would fit into the glass. His arm paused above Imogene's wine glass and it was then that he realized.

I guess you'll have to leave Russ.

What?

Benny put the half-carafe down. The waitress was hovering near the cash, seemingly afraid to come closer and afraid to leave.

Well, you will.

This wasn't really the way Imogene had imagined the conversation. She'd imagined it while she waited for the home pregnancy test to work. Home pregnancy? Where else would you privately confirm your pregnancy? What a stupid name, she decided and held a small wand up to the bathroom window. She guessed it couldn't be called a Work Pregnancy Test, and imagined a thousand women in office bathroom cubicles peeing onto white wands or into little trays and then holding things up towards the fluorescent lights. Outside the locked stall doors, the line-up just grew and grew as more women came in to see if they were pregnant.

The blue and white bathroom curtains bordered the wand. It was blue she was waiting for, she thought. Or was it not blue?

If I am pregnant, then what?

An inn on a lake. A huge room with a canopy bed. A balcony. Mountains. Okay, there's the where. With Benny, of course. Doing what? Talking about the child we are going to have. Picking names.

This is nuts.

What? said Benny.

This, sitting here in Rosetta's talking about how I'm pregnant.

Imogene imagined herself in her bathroom again, that afternoon, before she'd called Benny at the garage to see if he could meet her for dinner. She wasn't supposed to call him at the garage. He didn't say that, she did. It was one of her rules. But she'd called anyway. Five o'clock, she'd said, before Rosetta's gets busy.

Martha's got to work late anyway, he said, till ten.

For three months they'd met or tried to. It wasn't always easy for Benny. But Russ was away, and Imogene could always get there since Benny had stopped the smoking thing her car did.

It wasn't smoke, said Benny the first time they went to bed in her apartment.

It wasn't?

It was steam. Your rad. Smoke is worse, trust me.

Benny had said he'd fix her car first thing in the morning, and did she need a ride home from the garage?

Imogene of course needed a ride home. Benny seemed to know where she lived, even though they hadn't talked since he'd climbed over her parents' fence one ancient afternoon to say that he and Martha Loach were getting married. Martha went to their high school but Imogene didn't know her well. She hadn't known Benny did.

Why? Imogene wanted to ask there by the fence. Instead she asked, Do you want a Coke?

Looking back, as she often did, she realized this had probably seemed like a rude thing to say. But what the hell, she thought, was Benny doing?

Where's Russ? Benny asked as he opened his Coke and wobbled a loose fence board.

Up north, said Imogene. Surveying.

Lots of bugs there.

Yeah, I guess so.

You haven't talked to him?

Not really, not for a while. He left after …

She hadn't wanted to finish her sentence.

Graduation? said Benny.

Right.

Graduation always seemed to fuck you up, thought Imogene. She'd seen it happen to Peggy-Leigh, the year before. Peggy-Leigh's best friend Pam had been asked by Derek to graduation. Derek had been Peggy-Leigh's boyfriend for two years. It had been ugly. It was the first time Imogene really noticed her sister's habit of distractedly pulling hairs out of the top of her head, strand by strand.

Not to mention, Imogene continued remembering, the car accident the captain of the basketball team had, driving his graduation gift, a red convertible, into the lake.

And one of the cheerleaders had a kid nine months later. Lucy worked at the Beef and Brand as soon, she'd told Imogene, as she'd stopped breastfeeding and her mother took the kid.

Why Imogene ended up going to graduation with Russ, she didn't know. He'd asked her, not knowing about her and Benny, and anyway, she thought at the time, against her locker, with Russ looking right at her, what was there to know?

She'd never been able to hurt anyone. At least, not deliberately, she thought.

Sure, she said, I'd love to go with you. She tasted metal in her mouth.

Martha's dad owned the bait store. It was a thriving business, what with the town being on a lake. People came from everywhere to fish in the summer. Martha drove the minnow van. All summer Imogene watched the van drive up to Benny's to get him. She'd wave from her lawn.

Martha always smiled and waved back. But who wouldn't be happy driving a truck with Benny on the seat beside her? thought Imogene as she read another postcard from Russ.

Bugs are bad. Hot as hell. Having a great time. The guys are super. Why don't you come visit? Love Russell Innes, it was signed.

He still signs his last name, thought Imogene, turning the card over in her hand, like I won't remember which Russ.

The other side of the card showed evergreens and rocks. Russ was hoping to study geology at university. Imogene was hoping to avoid university. Benny was working in his father's garage. Martha drove a van full of minnows.

And gradually, Imogene and Benny had stopped talking. They both had work, they said, where did the time go? Imogene taught all those classes at the dance studio for Mrs Valente now that the woman's back wouldn't let her really instruct any more. She still tried to lead the class, but more often than not she retired to a chair in the corner and yelled out the steps, as Imogene, in front of the girls, demonstrated.

Eventually Mrs Valente retired completely, to the other side. The other side of the one-way mirror. When they first got the mirror, parents used to come in to see how good little Gina was, their six-year-old they expected big things from. Inevitably Gina was overweight, slow, and self-conscious. Or mothers came in to see if the money was really worth it. A lot of them decided it wasn't. And there were those parents who'd heard that their girls, ten years later, would walk better and would have longer muscles which would make them look like models and they'd get better husbands and then there would be no university costs to worry about. Imogene watched all these parents, and tried to slot them. She tried to be extra kind to the girls. Mrs Valente reached under her desk near the one-way mirror and pulled out a small bottle.

What will you tell Russ?

Imogene sighed and longed for some red wine. She sipped her water. The truth, she said.

Which is?

At first this seemed like a really stupid question to Imogene. But as she tried to talk, she realized how smart Benny was and that she'd always loved him. She started to cry.

Jesus, said Benny leaning over the table and wiping Imogene's face with his napkin.

Don't, said Imogene pulling away. My mascara will ruin the cloth.

That's what I love about you, said Benny.

Imogene couldn't be certain what he was referring to. Could it be that she wore mascara, never leaving the apartment without it? Ballerinas never went without make-up, she'd learned from Mrs Valente when Imogene was ten and was auditioning for summer classes at the National Ballet School in Toronto.

Marry me.

Imogene stared at him.

You're married, she said. Martha, remember? And looked at her watch.

That's been over for ages.

Imogene put down her water.

Benny continued talking with his eyes down, looking in the direction of the fettucine the waitress had brought.

She can't have kids.

Imogene looked at her ravioli. She'd ordered it out of habit. In high school they'd had a dance where the girls had to ask the guys to it, and had to take the guys to dinner before. Imogene had asked Benny and had taken him to an Italian restaurant that went under shortly after. Imogene ordered spaghetti and realized her mistake even before it arrived. The strands were suddenly lethal to her white blouse. And she knew pasta wasn't supposed to be cut. How can I talk and eat? Why are things between males and females so difficult, she wailed in her mind while pouring more Parmesan to kill time.

We tried for a year. Then she went to see a doctor. Impossible, he told us. That was it. It's her, not me, he added. Then he blushed. Obviously, it's not me.

He put his hand over Imogene's. Hers was covering a stain on the tablecloth.

Anyway, we kind of couldn't get over it. We'd never counted on just being the two of us. In fact, I think we got married because we both wanted kids. Not because we were in love.

Benny poured more wine.

Does this bother you? he asked.

No, no. I just can't believe we're talking like this.

I meant the wine, said Benny. Does it bother you if I drink and you can't?

I love you.

Benny's hands still had grease on them in places. Imogene stared at the black patterns. She wondered if they could be read like tea leaves. She imagined Benny washing his hands the way he did before they made love. They'd sit in the bathtub in the house he shared with Martha. Dark turquoise. They'd soak and talk and not talk about some things. As Imogene was drying off with a towel that more often than not said Benny and Martha, Benny would wash his hands again in the sink. Again and again.

It's okay, Imogene would say.

But Benny would say, I want you to know they're clean.

I do.

They were not like Russ's hands, thought Imogene in bed as she waited for Benny. Russ's hands often had small cuts in them from rocks he'd picked up. He was always talking about samples. Sometimes Imogene felt like she was one. Like he would slice her through the middle to see where the lines went.

I'm fool's gold, she'd think, lying alone in their bed when Russ was away. And he's out looking for the real thing.

He was away more than he was home. And he was happy. She'd never met anyone happier. Why was I afraid to say no to you, she thought. You could have handled it. Better than Benny.

She had thought about Benny a lot. And she knew he was still around. She assumed he knew she was still around. And neither tried to contact the other. Her father, Ray, had got them back together by giving her his old Mustang.

I'm too old to have something like this, he said. And it's too old to waste out there on blocks with a tarp over it. Don't know how well it runs, but it should be yours.

Was he just talking about the car?

And then her father had given her a one-arm hug that said, Come on kid, get your life in gear.

But she hadn't. Except she did stop reading the postcards Russ sent to their apartment from foreign countries. Or the north. What was the point? Still, she couldn't call Benny. There was Martha to think about. All those minnows.

Martha, said Benny, as the waitress asked about coffee for Benny and herbal tea for Imogene, always figured it was something I brought home from the garage.

All that oil and gas, she'd say, can't be good for a body. You poisoned me.

People could say the cruellest things to each other without even knowing what they'd done, thought Imogene. She and Peggy-Leigh had said some pretty horrible things growing up. It was funny, she thought, that Peggy-Leigh was the first person she thought of telling, other than Benny, when the home pregnancy test turned positive. She will be happy and she will help me, Imogene thought. This is good.

Peggy-Leigh had moved away the second she could after graduation. Who could blame her? And her frequent letters were like those from someone Imogene had never met. They wrote often. Peggy-Leigh was married and she and her husband lived in downtown Toronto.

I called Peggy-Leigh, said Imogene. She says hello.

She knows?

Everything. And she said Martha was never good enough for you and doesn't graduation fuck up lives?

Benny laughed.

I can make this man happier, thought Imogene.

Moments later Benny said, With you, in a winterized cottage on the lake, with our daughter. And we're sitting on the bed watching the snow and eating ice cream.

Either I told him this long ago, Imogene thought, or this is for real.

The Truth

•

Janis didn't think her mother did it to her on purpose. In fact, she
was pretty sure her mother was trying to prepare her, even at birth,
for the real world, so that she, unlike the singer she was named after,
would learn the truth, not at seventeen, but in an instant there under
the white delivery-room stars and the meteoric explosions of forceps
and other instruments clanging together.

Janis was named after Janis Ian, her mother would patiently recite
whenever the girls needed to hear that kind of thing. Janis Ian was a
folk singer who sang beautiful sad songs. And you were named after
Peggy-Lee, another singer, and Imogene was named after an actress.

Somehow this would always seem unfair to the two named after
singers. Do singers get to be on TV and in movies as often as
actresses? asked Janis, once. Hearing 'not really' was all it took for
the girl to think she knew the truth, just like in the song her mother
played when her father went fishing at night, that said everything in
life went to beauty queens. After all, thought Janis, I can't think of
any Miss Americas who just sing. During the question part they
always say they want to act. Or save the world, which always
sounded way too ambitious to Janis.

Was it life or love? Janis tried to remember as she hummed the
song while replacing silver hangers on the shiny chrome rack. Why
can't shoppers put things back the way they find them? Janis asked
her reflection in one of the twenty shop mirrors. Too late, she realized she'd looked in the mirror specifically made for skinny people.
Her hips stretched out to meet her stare, like an over-eager relative
you aren't sure about. This mirror was designed to make the under-
developed woman or teenager feel sexy. On the wrong figure, like
Janis's, which was womanly enough thank you, the mirror acted
more like an auditory aid. It said, Attention shoppers, here come
Janis's hips, breasts, and oh look, as she flees there is her bum.

A slow morning, thought Janis. And I'm losing my mind.

Life and love are just too close, she said. She often talked to herself when the store was empty.

Pardon?

Apparently, said Janis, I'm not alone.

A short woman was pulling her arm back from reaching for a blouse high up.

I can get that for you, offered Janis wielding a long pole. Even big people like me can't reach those racks, I don't know who they designed this store for.

Immediately she realized she'd committed sin number 7a in the Bible guide to selling, a red binder kept under the cash. She'd called attention to the shopper's flaw, the vulnerable spot like the soft circle on a baby's skull you are never supposed to touch. Janis had just spent the weekend watching too much television. It seemed there were a billion shows for parents. Didn't there used to be a lot of programs about home renovation and decorating? What happened to those? Who wants to know so much about breastfeeding and poop? Janis asked her plants. Looking closely at the television screen, you could see the unformed patch on top of a baby's head moving up and down with each breath.

The short shopper glared at her. I was just looking, she said.

Still, she took the floral blouse from the pole Janis handled like a fishing rod. She was a good fisherman, having done lots in Bay Lake. Look, she wanted to say, I hooked a rayon trout.

Again, expertly, Janis used the pole and steered the woman away from the mirror she was headed for, over to one for short, fat people. No getting around it, the Bible didn't have nice names for the mirrors, and this was the short fat one. Tall Scrawny, Acne Frizz, Old Bald, were three of the others.

I don't make the names, or believe in them, Janis would hum to herself, I just work here.

Janis had worked at Cash and Clothed for the past two years and she hated to admit it, but she loved her job. She didn't think you were supposed to enjoy retail as much as she did, so she told few people how she felt. Jeffrey knew, and didn't understand, but most of the time it was enough for Janis that he knew. Peggy-Leigh and Imogene, her sisters, knew and understood, or pretended to, but

Janis didn't see them often. Peggy-Leigh's artistic projects and Imogene's dissolving marriage and her hinted-at affair kept the sisters out of touch lately. Janis told herself she understood and that she wasn't that lonely anyway, really.

Who could be lonely in Toronto? she wondered.

When Janis arrived there five years earlier, she thought she'd go crazy in the first month. Too many people, too many things to do, too many cars, clothes, houses and apartment buildings to look at. How could anyone take it all in? Janis saw everything, life, love, as a store. Only so much stock could come in, inventories had to be taken regularly, and a certain amount had to continually leave the store. That's how things worked, she was sure. And how could you know things were leaving your mind the way they should to make room for new images, styles, trends? She tried talking to Jeffrey about this the first time they had dinner.

It might be a mistake, she had thought that first night, but the second glass was already kicking in, only two sips into it, and she had to admit, she was wearing the right clothes.

Still, Toronto was a huge adjustment. Janis realized she actually missed being isolated. Willow Junction, near Bay Lake, had been its own little boat. The first fall in the bigger city, I miss missing stuff, she told Domino, her gay neighbour who lived across the hall.

He said, Yes. He said this as he shook his head. He often did this when they talked, his voice saying one thing and his body another, like they never got together really.

Like marriages, thought Janis. At least, like Russ and Imogene's. And maybe Peggy-Leigh's.

She didn't want to think about marriage and so she dumped a basket of socks. This was one of the things she liked to do in the shop when it was quiet. There were several things you were supposed to do when there were no customers; some were quite tiring and boring and difficult, socks were ideal. Beautiful pastel shades in one basket, rag wool in another. A third held patterned. There were eight baskets full, yes sir, yes sir, she thought. Lately Janis had fallen in love. With extra thick 95 per cent cotton, 5 per cent spandex ones, blue. They cost more, she'd tell anyone who'd listen, but you never go back after having the real thing.

Was it life or love? Socks or lovers? God, Janis thought, and it's only Monday.

As much as she liked her job, there were times when she wondered how she'd get through the work week, and her work week frequently changed. Sometimes she had a weekend, sometimes she didn't, or not when most people like Jeffrey had his. Sometimes that worked out for the best, since weekends were usually family times for most people.

The pastel socks reminded her of Easter eggs her mother hid in the back yard for the three girls long ago. Last time Janis had been home, late August, she had found one in the shrubs, which weren't really shrubs any more.

What do you call an evergreen, she asked Domino back in Toronto, when it's ten feet and was planted twenty years earlier in front of the front window?

Is this a riddle? asked Domino.

Shrub didn't seem to do it, Janis decided. These were trees, blocking everyone from seeing in or out of the living room. Why hadn't her parents cut them down? Or trimmed them at least.

What's this?

Janis's mother, Iris, stopped raking. What?

Janis frowned and held something in her father's work glove. It looks like a foil egg, doesn't it?

She walked over towards the small pile of leaves her mother was standing in. It looked like Iris was wading the way she used to in the lake at the cabin, twenty minutes from Willow Junction, when the girls were little and Iris was afraid they'd swim out past the tires. The tires had been submerged by Janis's father, Ray, to mark how far the girls were allowed to go. Every summer they were only allowed out to where the water met Janis' chin. This upset her two sisters, who by being older, were by nature taller. One summer, after a horror-movie-like growing spurt, the water only came up to the bottom of Peggy-Leigh's breasts and she refused to swim unless it was deathly humid.

You just don't get it, said Peggy-Leigh when Janis begged her older sister to dive from tire to tire, like they used to.

Janis didn't get it, whatever *it* was, and didn't understand why her sister had tried swimming a couple of times in a thick, bulky sweatshirt their father had won at a golf tournament for being the worst golfer. The first time Peggy-Leigh dove from the tire, she sank like the rowboat anchor. Janis, underwater, saw her sister have to push herself up from the bottom of the lake. She surfaced, straining and coughing, the orange sweatshirt now a rust colour and covered in sand and driftwood bits. Peggy-Leigh left the water, slowly, seemingly unable to lift her arms which were crossed over her chest.

Iris, who was called Iris by Janis, though the other girls called her Mom, kicked the leaves as if she too was remembering the warm water up to her knees, and the three girls sitting on the soft sand watching tadpoles, or watching Imogene as she peed through her bathing suit to see if the lake would turn yellow.

An egg? said Iris as if she didn't want to touch it.

Yeah, look.

Iris looked and then started flattening the pile of leaves she'd raked only to rake them again.

What's going on, Mom?

Janis and Iris were both startled at this, neither could remember when Janis had last said Mom.

I don't know, Iris began. Remember how you girls used to look for them Easter morning?

Twenty years ago?

Was it that long? said Iris trying to straighten one of the rake's spokes which wasn't bent.

Janis decided to let it go, just then, maybe her father would know how the egg got there.

The pink socks were the best, then the green, then blue, then purple. Janis lined them up at the bar which was where the cash register was. The store was mostly wood and metal, all shiny and slick and sleek. Designed to get the customer in and out quickly, smoothly.

A sea of tranquillity you float through, joked the district manager.

You don't realize your wallet has fallen out of your bathing suit.

The bar was constructed to look like a bar, like a bar you'd have drinks at, dance near, something familiar that you couldn't quite place, something that encouraged you to relax, and to not notice you were handing over three hundred and seventy-eight dollars for a terry bathrobe, a flannel shirt, and socks.

Janis decided since things were slow, she'd package some socks. Package was what the Bible said you did after closing the sale, after you of course had sold up. That is, you added a belt, or pin, or purse the customer didn't really need. Not that he or she necessarily needed anything, but you added something after the initial impulse to buy. It was the retail game, and if played right, according to the Bible and Janis truly believed this one, both the customer and service representative would win.

Packaging meant wrapping the purchase in brown paper and then tying the bundle with string. There was an exact science to this which escaped Janis so she practiced often.

I am a butcher, she'd say, this is meat. Chops, a pound of ground beef. How about liver? Liver is the hardest to wrap, thought Janis, though it should be easy.

Liver was socks, or a blouse. Pants were ground beef. Chops, a sweater. The bundles leaving the shop were supposed to look just like those from your neighbourhood butcher's – neat, clean, no frills, quality at a good price, something you trusted. Image was everything at Cash and Clothed. Janis understood.

Janis liked image. Not her own, in fact she avoided it at all costs. She liked beautiful images, arresting images, something with rich colour. It was inevitable, she thought, that she worked in a clothing store. Cash and Clothed was more than she'd hoped for – it sold household clothes as well – linens, curtains, cushions, lamps, candles, lanterns, rugs, ceramics, bells to hang on your walls. She often thought she could live quite happily in the store. The rattan bed was there, and she knew how comfortable it was, how right-sized it was for two in the whirl of passion. She looked at her watch. Just after ten, Jeffrey would be at his office.

People were forever sitting on the bed. She couldn't blame them.

If you were spending three thousand dollars on a bed, you wanted to know it would work. It did seem unfair to her that such things as beds couldn't really be tried out. And when you think about it, she'd said to the district manager, you spend a third of your life in bed. He looked at her strangely.

Preferably not alone, she'd wanted then to add. But who was she to talk. Rick, desperate bachelor that he seemed to be, possibly had company in bed more often than she did. When this kind of thought occurred to her, Janis would say quietly but definitely out loud so that her conscience would hear, It's quality, not quantity. Jeffrey gave her as much time as he could. He said. And weren't they happy?

Weren't they happy?

He usually asked this in bed. After. And who could argue then? Janis wondered if they should have this conversation fully clothed, in an air-conditioned loan officer's office, say. Some place a little less comfortable, a little less romantic. Image, Janis thought, affects us more than we know. Her namesake knew all about it, Janis thought, and it's been passed down to me. What was my mother thinking? Janis Ian sings about being a sad loser, let's face it.

The bed in the store had been one time only. Inventory. When the shop was closed on a Sunday. Before Jeffrey had knocked on the dark glass and had tried to peer through the paper taped to block the view, Janis had been ticking things off. One bathrobe. One wife. Two candle-chandeliers two kids. Big house. Big alimony. Marriage of fifteen years. Forty-five pairs of socks. When Janis looked in one of the mirrors, a Closed for Inventory sign topped her head like a crown. Should maybe be closer to the heart, she thought, as she heard tapping.

As she slid back the glass door to tell whoever it was to go away, Jeffrey offered a single rose. Yellow.

What does yellow mean?

They were out of red?

No, said Janis. I forget, but it does mean something, you know, something significant.

How about Claudia is visiting her mother at the airport. A stop-over for a couple of hours.

Janis wasn't sure he was referring to how long his mother-in-law was at Pearson International, or to the time they had this time.

The kids are at somebody's cottage, he said before she could ask.

And the bed had been fabulous, if creaky. But the sound of rattan was soothing, not self-conscious-making.

Like making love in a pile of twigs in the woods but without the pain, said Janis afterwards. She thought she could smell fresh air on his skin. She sniffed his neck happily.

My mother used to do this when I was little and came in from playing outside. And my grandmother, she'd do it too. Especially in the winter. And my cheeks and nose would be really red, that colour.

Janis pointed to the rug on the wall.

Jeffrey looked. How *is* your mother?

He hadn't talked to Janis since before her last visit home. The beginning of the new academic year was always hectic – the kids, his new teaching schedule at the college, his wife usually had just finished showing a lot of houses and was busy at home sending cards and flowers to the new owners as they settled. He had warned Janis to expect a gap in communication and sex after Labour Day.

She even joked about it to Domino. She said, No sex right after labour, get it?

My mother? Janis reached for a pillow that had landed on the floor, and stuffed it under the three she already had her head on. Okay, I guess, I don't know, I found this egg.

An egg?

Yeah, you know, like a foil-covered one. It might have been chocolate.

So? I don't understand.

Neither do I, that's just it. And I'm not sure Iris does, that's the scary part.

Janis pulled the duvet up higher and lifted her chin over the covers.

She claims she doesn't know how it got there, the egg, where I found it in the tree shrubs, and I think I believe her. But she and I both have this weird feeling she should know why it's there. It's strange.

Jeffrey turned on his side to look at her. How much are these sheets? He fingered the cotton-lace edge.

Janis looked for a tag. Regularly three hundred, she said. He reached for his briefcase and then started to write her a cheque.

She started to cry.

What's wrong? He said, tipping the briefcase with his notes and text and spilling them on the Persian carpet beneath the bed. He gathered her up in a grip that reminded her not so much of an embrace, but of the way she was taught years ago by Peggy-Leigh to pull someone in from the water if they were drowning.

It's like you're paying me for sex.

What?

You know, we make love, and then you write a cheque?

It's for the sheets, he said. I thought we should buy them now, it's the right thing to do.

This struck her as oddly funny, and she started to laugh.

Now what? he said.

Janis was realizing she could either touch bottom or swim on her own anyway. He opened the net of his arms and she, like a goldfish, bobbed away.

You're thinking about the right thing to do? she asked. Okay, I know, and it's sweet and considerate of you not to let me pay given the size of my salary as compared to that of a professor, Janis said, trying to stop mirth, but the right thing to do would have been for you not to come to the shop today, not to get into bed with me, not to make me feel like I'm happier than I've ever been.

This last part seemed to surprise them both.

Jeffrey reached for his pants. I should go, my dearest. He reached back to kiss her on the top of her head. After all, he said, it's only a stopover, not a stay.

And then he was gone. The glass door slid behind him with the finality of an avalanche. Sometimes it doesn't feel like this, thought Janis as she turned to strip the bed, why does it hit when it hits? But she didn't wait for an answer, instead, she turned to the shelves of sheets and selected a colourful floral pair, as far from the ivory ones she had just become owner of, as she could get. She looked at the sheets in her arms – they were luxurious, clearly the best she would have in her apartment, but they would be too big. Her double bed would force her to wrap the corners of the fitted king sheet away like something to be hidden, something no one should see.

Her mother knew about Jeffrey. After six months of meeting in restaurants and then dashing back to Janis's apartment for an hour or two at most, Janis had had to tell. Jeffrey was that wonderful, that great of a deal, she thought, and she needed to have someone else agree. Talking to Domino made some things seem real, but not everything. And talking to her sisters wasn't really possible just then. Her older sister Peggy-Leigh was going through a difficult transition period in her art, she said, and Janis's other sister, Imogene, seemed to be having marriage troubles. On the other hand, Janis sometimes thought, Imogene didn't seem to be having any marriage troubles. She had no problems at all, and no good discoveries as far as marriage was concerned – Russ was always away, far away in the north where he said the rocks were amazing.

So she confided in her mother over lunch. Janis was home for the weekend and her mother had wanted to show her the newest restaurant near Willow Junction.

The bathroom, actually, said Iris once they got there. I want you to see the bathroom.

This didn't surprise Janis. Bathrooms had become a centre of interest for her family during a car trip to Florida when the girls were young. Peggy-Leigh, or was it Imogene? One of them had announced at a Denny's or a Howard Johnson that she was going to write a book about restaurant bathrooms.

They have music in there, said the sister, it's really neat.

Years later, in the Four Seasons Hotel in Yorkville, one of the first Toronto areas to seduce Janis, she burst out laughing in the ladies' room near the lobby and dining room. This would be their first dinner. Some sort of conference – MAL – she thought it was, and wasn't that the French word for sick? she wondered as she put on more pink lipstick and then took it off again with a Kleenex from a delicate gold box. There was a whole row of delicate gold boxes lined up in the wall of mirrors. Something familiar sang in the air. A ballet maybe, something she vaguely remembered her sister Imogene dancing to.

In a white tutu, a solo. Janis wished she could remember which sister had been taking notes on bathrooms, she would call her and say, This one should definitely be in.

A woman rushed in and dropped a binder heavily on the counter near one of the many black sinks. Who reads all this stuff? she asked Janis.

Janis smiled realizing the woman thought she was attending the conference there at the hotel. Oh, she said, you must be going to the MAL sessions.

The woman looked up from reapplying her blush. MAL? Then she started laughing. You mean MLA, she said between laughing more, although, she said, I think you got it right the first time. *Boring*. And there's more tonight and all day tomorrow. I don't think I can stand it.

Janis's heart sank. Not about the MAL thing, about the fact that maybe this was to be a short dinner with Jeffrey, this man she hardly knew, a meal between speakers, or workshops or whatever this conference was like. She only knew what retail conferences were like, having gone to one months before.

She hadn't wanted to go, which seemed only to convince her manager that she needed to attend.

Assistant managers needed to be fearless, among other things, Faye said, you'll learn a lot.

Can't I learn here? asked Janis, realizing how little she sounded, and worse, how small-town she sounded and she loathed that.

Only a week, said Faye. You'll love North Carolina.

Janis tried to block the memory, but it came roaring through, louder than the classical music in the washroom.

She was on the plane. An aisle seat beside two large men in army dress who were returning from the Gulf, they said and offered her a beer.

Have a Bud, one said, passing her a blue-and-red can as if it was a flower.

Janis looked at her watch. Nine-thirty. She was more in the mood for a morning coffee.

For us, said the other guy, our safe return.

The stewardess passed just as Janis was opening her beer.

Which attendant already brought out the beverage cart? she wanted to know. It's too early, she ...

But something stopped the woman mid-sentence. One of the men smiled and said. Aw, c'mon, we've been up all night flying back from Turkey and we still got a ways to go.

It's okay, said the stewardess quickly, just keep it down until we start serving the rest of the plane in a while.

Janis wondered if the same thing had stopped the flight attendant as had stopped her from refusing the beer and from refusing to talk to these strange travellers in her row. Death. Janis was sure both the men had seen someone die, sometime in the past months. She was terrified one of them would start to tell her about it. This fear at least took her mind a bit away from her fear of flying. But, she thought, I can't hear about death while I'm up here worried about dying in a plane crash. That's too much. Maybe the beer would help.

Where are you going? The man by the window asked. And do you want to sit here? He started to get up.

Horrified, she waved him back down and spilled a bit of beer in the process. No, no, I don't like flying, I don't want to see.

The men thought this was funny, since, they said, they always flew, and usually while seated backwards, and sometimes it was bad. They soon backed off with their telling and actually, thought Janis, tried to take her mind off being afraid.

So where are you going? the other one asked.

Boone, North Carolina.

'Team Building' was the name of the conference. And the people attending would all be from the stores owned by Cash and Clothed's parent company. There would be shoe stores, men's clothing stores, fitness shops, and shops like Janis's. Managers, assistant managers, and owners would be the participants. Janis felt ill every time she reread the brochure.

Yes, she'd told Faye, I want to have a future with the company. But I'm very happy being assistant manager here, I don't want more, I don't want to manage the new store. I've only been here a short time, I like it. I don't want more.

The team-building was to take place at a small hotel on a hill heading up into the Blue Ridge Mountains. The location cheered Janis a bit when she arrived. Willow Junction barely had hills let alone mountains. And these really did look blue. One of the conference organizers, Mike, tried explaining it to her, something about all the trees and oxygen and would she like a closer look? He could drive her up a mountain path on their first free afternoon, Would you like that? he asked.

She hadn't had time to decline when another organizer, Ruth, told them to get with the group. Did you sign your release? she asked Janis.

My release?

This form, here, and remember, take off all your jewellery.

Then Ruth was gone, over to another group of nervous-looking retail team-builders. One of the men was talking about his wedding ring. I never take it off, haven't in seventeen years. I mean, would it be okay if I leave it on? Why do we have to have no jewellery?

You'll see, said Ruth smiling.

Must be with the fitness stores, thought Janis.

She signed her release, put on comfortable, flat shoes as had been specified, and joined the others outside the dining room. At least I don't have to worry about taking off a wedding ring, she thought, trying to keep her spirits up.

The man beside her smiled and said hi. He looked about as miserable as she felt so Janis liked him.

What are you in for? she asked.

Blaine, according to his name tag, laughed and said, Owner, almost apologizing.

He didn't look like an owner, thought Janis, too plain-looking, too normal, too nice. Not long, right? she said.

Last week. Thought I should find out what I bought and how to own it. My wife's always liked Cash and Clothed. He blushed when he mentioned his wife and Janis wondered why. How about you? he asked. Not married, said Janis.

No, I mean, and he blushed again, are you an owner?

Now she blushed. Oh, no, I'm just an assistant manager, Toronto.

Vermont, he said shaking her hand.

Usually she wasn't crazy about shaking hands, but Janis liked Blaine so far.

Good weather, he said.

Was this a salutation? she wondered. Like, Good luck?

Pardon me? she said.

Toronto, he said, good weather. I was a meteorologist in my past life, last week.

Ah, she said and was about to ask more when Ruth came back and chided them.

Okay, you've met now mingle with other people, and she gently pushed Janis away from Blaine. She took Blaine by the arm.

Janis followed a group around a parking lot. A huge college-aged student was leading them. His T-shirt said Razorbacks and made her nervous.

I'll be your host this afternoon, he was saying. Ever heard of Outward Bound?

Now she was afraid. Yes, she had heard of it. What seemed like a long time ago, Imogene's friend Benny had gone on an Outward Bound trip two years after his dirt-bike accident.

His doctor's idea – Benny thinks it's stupid, Imogene had told her, and so do I, we were gonna go camp at Martyn River.

Janis thought that was stupid, she didn't like camping – too many bugs, you had to worry about bears and what about lightning? She said this to Imogene, also trying to make her sister less disappointed about not going camping with Benny and Imogene had said, You don't get it. It's not about camping, stupid.

Benny had come back ten days later, furious. He wouldn't tell anyone the whole story.

Take you there and leave you there with not enough food and barely enough water and these other idiots who don't know how to do anything and whose rich parents sent them on this adventure and I get stuck looking after them.

And apparently, according to Imogene who asked to borrow Janis's new blue top to go to the movie the night Benny got back, one rich kid made fun of Benny's leg being shorter than the other one.

Still, Benny's the one who carried the canoe, said Imogene with what Janis thought was pride, like she'd carried it herself. No, I don't get it, Janis decided, handing over her top, just a couple of years ago Imogene wasn't speaking to Benny because he tricked her into seeing the fish he was gutting in the basement after ice-fishing.

And then Janis had seen Imogene and Benny kiss under the picnic table during hide-and-seek when Janis was it.

When you're older, Janis's mother would say. And she'd never finish her thought.

When I'm older, what?

Blaine somehow caught up with her and was right behind her, following Joe (but you can call me Boomer) into the woods.

Did he say Outward Bound?

Clearly, thought Janis, he thinks this is bad news too.

Better get out of here, said Janis. Ruth might see us talking. Blaine laughed. I hate these things. Worse than going to church when you have to shake your neighbour's hand and say, Peace be with you.

And also with you, answered Janis. If we have to form a circle and hold hands I'm out of here.

I dare you, said Blaine.

Janis smiled. Maybe this isn't going to be so bad, she thought.

Let's make a pact, she said to Blaine who was beside her now, whenever we need a partner let's work together.

You know they won't like that, said Blaine and was about to add something when Boomer barked at him.

Hey, you, you're outta line!

Line was the last word Janis heard.

Pardon? she asked the new woman in the glamorous hotel washroom.

Are you in line?

Janis realized it did look like she was waiting for a free stall. Oh, no, she said, Go ahead, I think they're all free.

What a conference, eh? the woman said to another binder-toting woman.

Let me tell you about a conference, thought Janis, thinking back on how they'd had to be blindfolded, every one of them except a guy named James (it would turn out there were six guys named James and one woman named Jamie so that by the last day, Blaine and Janis had convinced everyone to put a slash through their name plates around the conference big table and to write in JAMES) who would lead them into the woods.

You know, said Boomer, it's like the blind leading the blind, one leading many, it's supposed to be a metatarsal, I think.

People murmured in confusion. You mean metaphor? asked Janis trying to be helpful.

Why don't you tell us what I mean, said Boomer walking over near Janis who was still blindfolded. Suddenly he lifted her up, over his head she thought, and she screamed.

Hey, just seeing how you'll be on the next part, said Boomer putting her down. Ladies and gents, we have a winner here. Too bad you can't see her – she's real light. She's the one you're gonna wanna lift through the thing we call the spider web so she can put the rope ladder down for the rest of you.

What? thought Janis and she was pretty sure the other fifteen people in the group felt the same. She was terrified of spiders. And snakes.

Oh yeah, said Boomer as Janis held on to the person in front of her and stumbled deeper into the woods, as Blaine behind her held on firmly to her shoulders, having mistakenly touched her breasts when they were still lining up and trying to get going and had just been blindfolded.

Oh yeah, Boomer repeated.

Oh yeah, what? finally one of the Jameses asked.

Oh yeah, I forgot to ask, Is anyone allergic to snake bites?

At this, Janis and several others ripped off their blindfolds. How are we supposed to know if we're allergic if we've never been bitten? asked Blaine.

Janis was grateful Blaine seemed practical.

Well, said Boomer, we like to ask. We've got an anecdote kit anyway, he said.

Janis felt sick. She heard the word snake and then felt dizzy. Boomer was still talking. Something about cotton. A cotton snake? She

pictured cotton snakes her grandmother made to keep the cold out.
She placed them on the floor in front of doors. Janis's mother
refused them, she hated snakes, even colourful, embroidered and
quilted ones as nice as yours, she said. Janis thought she was afraid of
snakes because her mother was. And snakes seemed to find them –
once in Florida when Janis and her mother were walking behind the
other girls and their father – black and copper and curled under a
flowering bush – and once at the cabin – a Parry Sound rattler out of
its territory, at the base of the stairs up from the dirt road to the cabin
as Janis and her mother walked up from the lake. Janis's bare feet
almost stepped on the snake, but her mother screamed. Janis jumped
back, the snake moved and Janis's mother hit it with the shovel she'd
grabbed from the shed earlier that afternoon, having wanted to rake
some of the weeds out of the water.

Somewhere in the distance there was thunder.

Great, Janis said to Blaine who had tied his blindfold into a bow
tie, now all of my fears are in one place.

Spiders, snakes, and the third? Blaine was trying to make Mickey
Mouse ears with Janis's blindfold and was pulling the knot too tight.

Ow. Thunder.

I can fix that, Blaine said in a whisper as Boomer explained the
next event to the rest of the unhappy group. Remember, until last
week, I was a meteorologist. Thunder is just …

Lightning, she interrupted. Thunder is not the problem, lightning is. Especially for people in the woods.

Can you believe they are making us use e-mail?

The woman named Fran said this to the other conference-goer.
Janis couldn't read her name tag. Fran's handwriting wasn't much
better and at first Janis thought her name was Flan.

How can they make us do things we don't want to do?

Is there a guy named Boomer here? Janis asked.

Both women stood back from the mirror and their lipsticks and
looked at her.

Just a man I met at a conference a while back, said Janis digging
through her purse for her lipstick to show that she belonged.

Even, she said as she began to dump things out onto the vanity, when I said I was terrified of lightning and wasn't the thunder coming closer, he just laughed at me.

The two women stared.

Really, Janis continued as she picked fuzz off mints and put them back in her purse, I gave him a chance to surrender with dignity, I wasn't trying for a mutiny, in fact I really didn't care about anyone else there except maybe Blaine and I had just planned that when I couldn't stand it any more I'd run back to the hotel.

What are you talking about? asked Fran.

Team Building, a conference.

Oh, said the other woman, I heard about that one, it's Writing Across the Curriculum, right? That'll never work.

Janis didn't know what that was.

Are you going to the closing wine and cheese? Fran asked the other woman.

We had a potlatch, interrupted Janis.

A what?

The last night, said Janis, half sitting on the vanity close to Fran, we were supposed to meet in the lounge and everyone in the group would give a gift to the group. Blaine and I dreaded it the whole week. Every day on our schedule, the printing seemed to get darker and bigger: *Potlatch, potlatch, potlatch*.

The other woman was listening too.

I couldn't think of a gift, wasn't even sure what they meant, in fact I had no idea right up until I heard Blaine give his gift.

A woman came in and walked to a stall.

He was a meteorologist, right? Well, he gave everyone the forecast for their own area for the next day. He went one by one, and gave mine last. He told me I'd have no turbulence, no cloud, I could have kissed him.

The new woman came out of the stall, washed her hands slowly, as if waiting for the story to resume. Janis didn't care.

So I volunteered to go next. I kind of stole from his idea – I gave everyone a colour they should try wearing. I'd been watching everyone's clothes all week and couldn't believe people in the business could be so wrong, so tame, so quiet. I thought if I just told one of the Jameses how great he'd look in grey, he'd be set. And one woman was screaming for brown and she only wore blue. So I looked each person in the eye and said Red, Blue, Green, Taupe, Black, Yellow, Off-white, White. Of course I repeated the colours, depending on what was needed.

The three women at the sinks looked at Janis. Then at their own clothes. No words were needed.

Then Janis said, Black. Black. Black.

The three smiled back.

Eventually Janis left the elegant washroom and searched for Jeffrey. Just after their appetizers and before the entrees it became clear that they would be spending the night together in room 603. Jeffrey had simply reached into his blazer pocket and pulled out the key and had placed it on the linen tablecloth between them. The action made Janis think of an engagement ring.

She knows the university booked me a room.

Janis had noticed in the few times they met Jeffrey never mentioned his wife by name. The children yes, Ivy and Jason.

The chair thought I should network as much as possible, since the registration fee is so outrageous. So we've got two nights, if you'd like.

Of course she'd like, thought Janis. She'd love.

The bathroom, her mother was saying, you've got to see it. I think your shop could carry some of the wicker.

What? Sorry, Iris. Janis knew she'd been caught daydreaming. I was thinking about something at work.

Her mother sipped her water. Is he still married?

Janis jerked up from the menu. Yes.

How did you say you met him, the store?

Yes, he was buying his wife a scarf for her birthday.

What kind of a gift is that? her mother wanted to know.

It was a silk scarf, said Janis defensively and then wondered what she was doing. She *had* thought it a strange gift when the man explained he needed a last-minute gift for his wife's fortieth birthday and did she think it was a good choice? He held up the scarf the way a little boy would hold up his elbow having fallen off his bike. Domino's nephew did that exact gesture and it broke Janis's heart.

She thought it was a very nice scarf, in fact, the day the shipment arrived, she'd selected the richest one – red and blue – and had set it aside as her own purchase. With her discount it was sixty dollars. Too much for a scarf, she thought, and too much for her budget, but the colours took her somewhere. And besides, she reasoned, the scarf fit her criteria. In her latest effort to stop herself from buying more clothes from the shop, she tried to limit herself to buying things for the apartment. And when she wasn't wearing the scarf, she could drape it over an end table or a bedroom dresser, or she could delicately pin it to the wall. Not near the door though, she thought, Domino would want it as soon as he saw it.

Be a love, he'd say. Just for tonight. I won't spill wine, I promise. And I'll be careful not to burn a hole in it.

But I just got it, she'd say already knowing she'd say yes.

He's a lawyer, Domino would say, as if that explained everything. I'm an actor, for god's sake.

A scarf *was* good for a first impression. Not especially good when you'd forgotten your wife's fortieth birthday. Janis knew this but decided to say nothing. As she rang in the sale, she tried to unravel why she hadn't told him.

Had she wanted this man to be in trouble with his wife?

Had she wanted him to like her, a sales technician as the Bible called them, for reassuring him and for applauding his choice, his taste?

Did she realize she couldn't bear to tell him no, about this or anything he might ask her now or later?

He wrote a cheque and passed it to her. When her eyes met his he looked down.

Janis reached for a small bottle of perfume from the shelves behind her.

This comes with any scarf, she said, I should have mentioned it earlier. Should I wrap these together?

There, she thought, his wife will be less upset. Perfume. Rats, she thought. Why did I have to do that? She read the bottom of the bottle, Passion. Nope, she thought, and reached for another.

Jeffrey Warren looked at her. Jeffrey Warren who lived at 148 Roselawn Crescent.

I don't like this one as well. It's a bit strong, she lied. This other is much nicer.

Mock Orange, she read to herself. That will do.

And Jeffrey had left with a brown-wrapped parcel that looked from the outside like chicken livers.

She hoped that his wife wouldn't be too furious to open the gift. It wasn't a bad gift. And she didn't want him to be in trouble necessarily, she just didn't think she wanted him to be happily married.

What am I doing? She asked Faye who breezed back from her fifty-minute ten-minute break.

Running a shop? suggested Faye.

Running something, said Janis.

Faye looked at her.

Socks, she'd go to the socks, it was time to mix the types and the colours rather than keep them in their separate baskets, thought Janis. And she hummed about beauty queens with clear-skin smiles and thought that Jeffrey Warren's wife must be one.

The waiter passed by and said, Hello, Iris.

Janis's mother smiled and slid back into her seat. She'd just returned from the restaurant's washroom, having been gone for over fifteen minutes. Janis had started to worry just before Iris returned – maybe it was the bleeding again, so unpredictable.

Like weather, her mother had said recently.

Janis had tried to reassure her and had said, Could you think of it as a front moving through, something temporary, bringing clear skies with it?

Iris had looked at her. What?

I had this friend once, a meteorologist. At a conference actually, and every time the facilitators suggested something stupid, Blaine would say, Patchy fog bringing with it heavy rain. Or, Look for a clearing trend.

Sounds pretty rude, said her mother frowning and putting on her glasses to read the menu.

No, no, he wasn't like that. I was the only one who heard him. He made the conference something I could stand.

Iris still wasn't convinced. She lifted her water glass and held it like a flashlight on Janis.

Well, I liked his sense of humour, she tried explaining. He called the leaders Hurricane Mike, and Tropical Storm Ruth. And, she continued and laughed, Boomer was the tornado that spun itself out over the sea.

Boomer? What kind of conference *was* this?

Not as interesting as it sounds, said Janis. Retail. Why were you gone so long? asked Janis, changing the subject. I had time to inventory the whole place, it's quite lovely.

I thought you'd like it here, her mother smiled. You've got to see the ladies' room.

You've said that, said Janis.

To dry your hands? They've got neatly rolled white washcloths. Must be fifty of them. And then you drop them into a white wicker basket – there's a lid. It's very tidy.

Sounds creative, said Janis, suddenly hungry. Can we order? She'd forgotten how hungry she'd been when they'd entered through the French doors. She'd been distracted when her mother took so long in the washroom. Lately her mother had complained of heavy bleeding. She wasn't even supposed to be having a period any more, really, she'd been wearing the patch for a couple of years.

I feel like a rubber raft, she'd said once to Janis when they were in the bathroom at home and Iris was drying off after the bath and applying an estrogen replacement patch. I'll leak if I don't stick this on.

Janis sat on the toilet cover looking confused.

Or a balloon. Maybe that's it. I'll spin off wildly if I don't seal things.

Are you having trouble with this? asked Janis, reaching for an Avon catalogue so as not to appear to be prying. She was never sure lately how much privacy her mother wanted. She hadn't thought about it at all when she was a kid – she loved sitting in the bathroom while her mother bathed – the bath oil fragrance, or bubbles were so wonderful. And the warm air, trapped in the small room, made her feel good. It slow-motioned things, she'd once told her mother.

Her mother had stopped drawing the washcloth down her leg.

What?

Makes everything slow. It's so fast outside here, she'd tried to explain.

They both could hear Peggy-Leigh and Imogene fighting about something.

You're too little, I'm not teaching you pig-Latin! Peggy-Leigh said as she slammed her bedroom door.

Imogene wailed outside it, I'm not too little!

Sometimes Janis followed the bath bead through the water. She thought the blue ones were best with the turquoise tub – she told her mother the red ones didn't go.

Well, some day, her mother had said, you can run a shop that sells these and you can advise customers on what colour they should buy for their bath.

Janis had thoroughly liked the idea.

She still sometimes sat in the bathroom while her mother bathed but she wasn't sure if she should. Would you tell me if I was doing something you didn't like, Iris?

Janis's mother looked over the top of the menu. Haven't I? she grinned. Didn't I used to say, Call me Mom?

Before Janis could answer, her mother said, I know, I know, and you were right way back then, it *did* distinguish you from your two sisters. They've never called me Iris. In fact, even your father doesn't.

What does he call you?

Mother, Iris replied, you know that. And then she asked, Do you have a tampon in case I need it?

Bleeding again? asked Janis.

I might be. Then she laughed, It's crazy, as if someone my age would want to have a kid!

Some women do, said Janis thinking of the last *People* magazine she'd read. A fifty-five-year-old woman in Italy gave birth to twins last year.

God, said her mother.

No, science, said Janis, drugs.

What I meant was, can you imagine someone my age being a good mother?

Sure I can, said Janis. You'd be a great mother at any age.

She liked trying to let her mother know she remembered things. It wasn't easy to tell her mother that she understood things now. Things like how the three girls and Iris would live at the cabin all week while Ray lived at home and worked. Every summer was like that. While the girls had played mermaid in the lake, or climbed the cliff behind the cabin, their mother had read hundreds of paperbacks and home-decorating magazines.

Why do you read those? Imogene had asked once with a hint of frustration. This place doesn't look anything like the magazines – we don't even have running water! And we've got an outhouse! And what are we supposed to do all summer! There's no one to play with! It's not like Benny's around or anything!

Thinking later, Janis thought Imogene was probably just mad because Peggy-Leigh wouldn't let her play Barbie with her and Janis. And still later, Janis thought it was probably because even then, Imogene was in love with Benny.

The spinach salads and French onion soups were quite good. Janis and her mother were both overcome with giggles when the melted cheese roped itself between bowl and spoon and hung in the air like Christmas tinsel. People were starting to stare. This often happened to Janis and her mother when they were out together.

Check out the bathroom while I pay the bill.

Let's split it, said Janis.

No, sweetie. My treat. You've got your big Toronto rent to pay, and besides, your father gave me some money this morning. I told him we needed groceries.

Then she finished her glass of white wine while Janis waited for the rest of the story.

We don't.

Don't what?

Need groceries, her mother said. But I wanted to take you to lunch and to go shopping. There's this new shop you've got to see – it's got furniture and drapes and the neatest cushions. They're shaped like moons and stars.

So Janis headed for the ladies' room and felt slightly sad. She'd never liked that her mother had to lie to her father for money. And it hadn't had to be that way, really. After the three girls had started high school, Peggy-Leigh just finishing as Janis started, Iris had wanted a job. A paying job she corrected Ray, when they'd begun and ended discussing it. He didn't want the girls to suffer. What if one of them was sick at school and wanted to come home? he said. He didn't have an office job – he worked out of the MTO, Ministry of Transportation Office, driving various vehicles – trucks, sanders, whatever was needed.

It had been the same in the summers. While Iris did love being by the lake, she must have missed Ray, thought Janis, missed being a complete family. And did sometimes miss warm water, her sporadic opportunities to have bubble baths. Missed feeling connected somehow, rather than isolated by cliff on one side, lake on the other. Weekends probably went too fast for her, and it seemed to Janis when she looked back that Iris never got enough time with her husband – as if she didn't want to deprive the three girls of any second with their father.

Lately she'd started telling Janis things, like how sometimes she felt she had to choose between children and the man she loved. It was hard for Janis to hear. Then she thought, No, it's hard to know what to say.

She loved both her parents, and, being one of three girls, was trained to see two sides to everything – as Janis was growing up, one side was Peggy-Leigh's, the other was Imogene's. But more and more she was starting to see things the way her mother saw them. Maybe it's because I'm getting close to thirty, thought Janis, as she opened the ladies' room door.

Blue, white and brass. Very restful, and decadent at the same time. She didn't have to go to the bathroom, not in the literal sense, so Janis just looked at everything and wondered, What does she want me to see? While the room seemed lovely, Janis had this sense that there was something specifically in the small room which locked that her mother felt she needed to become aware of.

She looked in the white wicker mirror. Her lipstick was still on, amazingly enough. Her mother had been right. The seventeen-dollar lipstick *was* worth it. All those articles Iris read weren't lying, thought Janis, smiling her Don't Tell Plum grin.

Then she decided to wash her hands, get the cheese smell off her fingers, which finally had had to wind a rope or two into her mouth. Fifty or so white facecloths rolled so they looked like pale jellyrolls, thought Janis as she reached for one in the middle of the stack. Could be wood, she thought before she touched the cotton, white little logs stacked as neatly as her father stacked. And suddenly she longed to stack wood with him.

Something fell out of the facecloth. In Janis's vision it was a shiny pink blur. It rolled across the dark blue ceramic tile.

Janis reached under the white wicker hamper.

An egg. A small foil-wrapped ball. When Janis held it to her nose, sure enough, it smelled like chocolate.

Her mother.

How could she know I'd reach for that one?

She stared at the other rounded cloths. She pulled one, and there it was, a green egg. Pulled another, a blue egg. One by one, the soft facecloths were unrolled by Janis, and each one contained a foil-covered chocolate egg.

That's what took her so long, thought Janis. What is she doing?

She realized she'd have to leave the washroom and rejoin her mother. But she wasn't sure she wanted to – she wasn't sure she wanted to know what was going on, at least, not yet. Maybe she could talk to her father. Maybe he'd noticed things. As she left the ladies' room, she made up her mind not to let on to her mother about the eggs. She'd neatly plopped them into a brass bowl on one of the wicker shelves near the sink, not wanting to carry close to fifty chocolate eggs in her purse, not wanting to carry anything until she knew what it meant.

She tried to fix the right expression on her face as she met her mother outside the restaurant.

Ready?

For what? asked Janis apprehensively.

That new store. The moon and stars, remember?

I think something's wrong with Iris, said Janis.

Jeffrey pulled the terry robe he was wearing closer around himself. He retied the knot. It was her white robe.

You mean she's ill?

Well, not physically, said Janis. At least, no more than her usual menopause stuff.

Bleeding again?

Jeffrey knew most of the stories. After every visit with her parents, Janis would fill him in eventually.

No, I think that's okay. In fact, Ray seems to think it's stopped finally.

You and your dad talk about things like that?

Like what? Janis sat down across the table for two and looked out the window. The park was losing its leaves. Soon the people in the highrise on the other side of the park would be able to see into her apartment. Jeffrey wouldn't want to sit in the window any more, not till summer. She thought he was being paranoid now. She used to find it exciting, slightly mysterious, the way they lived. Lately it seemed just to annoy her.

We miss so much, she'd tried to tell him last winter. The skaters, the pick-up hockey. At night the trees have little white lies.

She'd meant to say lights. Lies had upset Jeffrey and he'd said he wouldn't talk about it any more and would she sit with him over on the couch? Janis knew he liked the living room – it had no windows whatsoever. It reminded her of a blue cave.

Like reproduction, Jeffrey said pulling the blind but leaving the slats open.

Ah, yeah. I mean, I don't think it's always easy for Ray to talk about some things, but you know, you sometimes have to.

Well, I can't imagine talking to Ivy about that kind of thing.

Ivy is fourteen, said Janis.

Meaning what?

Meaning, said Janis, reaching for the bagels and lox Jeffrey had brought, I don't think you'll have to have the father-daughter talk about serious menopause and the possibility that Claudia may experience Alzheimer's at some future date.

Jeffrey flinched as if he'd cut himself with the knife while he was slicing a bagel for her.

Can we not talk about her? he said and dangled half a bagel on the end of the knife like a bribe.

Darn, said Janis.

Jeffrey's distinguished grey eyebrows went up.

About the poppy seeds, said Janis. I like plain. The seeds stick between my teeth. Sure, I mean, your wife and family are not really my favourite thing to talk about. On the other hand, we can't pretend they don't exist?

Can't we? smiled Jeffrey with his adorable smile, standing up and sliding a hand up underneath the wide sleeve of the satin kimono he'd given Janis for her last birthday. He'd joked about how he'd learned his lesson about scarves for birthdays, and had asked how could she have let him go to his wife with that gift? What was she thinking? he wanted to know.

I wasn't thinking, Janis had said, blushing. I was feeling.

He put his arm around her, steered her into the next room. He sat down and pulled her back into him.

She saw herself as a red flotation device thrown to the drowning. Peggy-Leigh had told her she should always circle the victim first.

Talk to him, she'd said. Keep your leg out as you tread water. He may try to pull you down, so be ready to kick him.

Who knew, thought Janis, my sister was teaching me to save my own life, not someone else's.

And Janis thought about how Peggy-Leigh had made her practise. Janis would tread water with her back to her sister who would be the victim. The water would be bottomless. At some point Peggy-Leigh would attack her from behind and pull her under and hold her there. Janis was supposed to practise one of her breaks before she swallowed too much water or blacked out.

They curled into one end of the striped couch.

This signals the end of our broadcasting day, she mused silently, the end of real talk. But I'm tired anyway.

I think maybe Iris is just going through something, she said. And so does my father, we're just not sure what.

Janis caught herself looking for little eggs in the socks at work.

Oh, boy, she thought, my mother is getting to me. But even worse, she realized, I'm disappointed at not finding an egg.

Must be my period, she told herself, but then realized she might have said it out loud because two customers were looking at her.

Her period was ending. Soon she'd start the next little packet of birth control pills. Or would she? she wondered. It was all very new and confusing, this feeling she'd really only noticed in the last few months, and hadn't been able to ignore in the last week. She figured it was the culmination of several things. Not in order, she listed them on a pad near the cash register.

Mother and menopause. Chocolate eggs. Jeffrey's conference in Halifax this weekend. Fishing. New shipment.

She looked at the boxes near the back of the store. It wasn't like her, she realized, not to unpack them right away. After all, she hummed to herself two mornings ago when the boxes began arriving, the Bible tells me so.

Unpacking immediately was one of the ten commandments.

You can't sell it if no one can see it, Rick would say as he made one of his unannounced fast visits to the store.

It's been here ten minutes, Rick, Janis would say. And I can't give you the run-down of what we've sold recently if I'm unpacking and ticking things off the packing slip at the same time, can I?

I'm sure *you* could, Rick would say, trying to flatter her so that he could minutes later try to get her to agree to a date. He never changed.

And really, thought Janis, once in a while I need the attention of a man who is desperate for me.

So she hadn't unpacked right away because Rick had arrived almost with the five large boxes. But even after he'd gone, Janis hadn't unpacked with her usual flurry and efficiency. Normally she couldn't wait. In the sometimes routine life of retail, new stock was a pleasure blown all out of proportion. Domino had told her this earlier in the week when she'd spent most of their evening tea hour chatting about the new things in her store.

Darling, he'd finally interrupted, look at yourself.

She did. The Victorian nightgown from the store looked lovely, she thought, like out of a magazine. Maybe even Victoria's Secret, she'd suggested to Domino.

Well, I guess, he reluctantly agreed and said, they *do* throw in five of those along with two hundred slutty, sexy things. I guess that's so prudish women will agree to have the catalogue home delivered.

Dom! she'd said laughing, that's mean.

But true, she thought.

Janis realized even she blushed a bit when she got her mail in the evenings and realized all the other tenants had probably already skimmed the magazine and then stashed it back in her mail slot.

What is she doing subscribing to this? she imagined they'd say. Who is *she* going to dress or undress for?

This, it turns out, was Domino's point exactly.

I come over here, he said, almost every night for our little tête-à-tête, and you waste my talent talking about the store.

Janis looked hurt.

Sweetie, he quickly went on, it's for your own good. Look at what you talk about. I want to talk about relationships, people, living, breathing, divine creatures like Chase.

Is that a real name?

Don't know, don't care. I'm over the moon.

Then he'd begun to sing 'The Ladies Who Lunch'. Janis liked this about her neighbour, he sang often, and he had a good voice. Really, you should be on Broadway, she said.

I should, agreed Domino, as he continued singing with a song from something he said was called *Oklahoma!* Something about a surrey and a fringe.

What's a surrey?

Not important, said Domino mid-song. But the fringe, my dear? I'm living on it.

Don't you want something more?

Nope, thanks, this is enough, said Jeffrey, putting his plate down on the blanket box coffee table in front of the couch. He reached for the remote.

Janis considered the sunflower-seed bread, the shaved ham, cheese, olives, and tomato wedges.

I wasn't referring to dinner, she said.

Jeffrey looked at her and then looked at the volume button.

She could see he really wanted to turn up the news. Probably he wants to check his stocks, she thought. She saw his thumb hover over the smooth triangle as if to say, It would be so easy for me to block out everything else and just hear what I want.

He sighed. What is it? he asked.

He asked, but not easily enough, thought Janis. Lately everything seemed to have significance for her.

This. I mean, I used to love our picnics, she said.

I thought this wasn't about dinner?

It isn't. Dinner is just a metaphor.

Oh, said Jeffrey turning the television off and facing her.

I just want more now. More than you just dropping over whenever it's 'okay' or 'possible'. I don't even know what those words really mean.

Jeffrey poured them both some more wine.

Should I have brought something other than ham? he asked.

No, Janis laughed. It's just, sometimes I'd like to know ahead of time when you'll be here. I'd like to be able to look forward to seeing you.

You don't?

Janis paused and fished a piece of cork out of her blue-green Mexican goblet.

No.

No?

Not in that sense.

And what sense *is* that? said Jeffrey with, thought Janis, a little panic in his voice.

Good, she thought, and then said, I don't look forward to seeing you because I can't let myself. What if I spent all day thinking about what I wanted to tell you or what I wanted to do with you?

He smiled at that.

And, she continued, you didn't show up for three days?

You could always call me.

At the office. That's real personal, she said, sounding, she realized, a little too much like people she knew where she grew up.

Janis.

They both put their glasses down.

Janis, what *is* all this?

I don't know, she half-groaned. I just want more than *this*, she gestured at the blue-and-white plates and bowls in front of her, and no, it's not about food and yet it is. What if I want to make dinner for you sometime?

Jeffrey laughed, You told me you can't cook.

Well, maybe I can't because I don't have to. I'd get better at it if I was cooking for us. Domino would love to help me.

I'll bet he would.

What's that mean?

Jeffrey dropped an olive pit onto the edge of his plate. I think you spend too much time with him.

What?

This came out a little louder than Janis or, it seemed, Jeffrey expected.

So, there is something there? said Jeffrey gulping some more Burgundy.

Are you kidding?

No.

Don't try to get this away from you and me.

I'm not trying anything. I want to know what he's trying.

He's gay, said Janis.

You're sure?

Well, shit. Janis had managed not to swear in front of Jeffrey before. How am I supposed to be sure? He doesn't try to get me into bed, if that's what you want for proof. But what does that prove, lots of straight men don't seem to be trying to get me into bed very often!

She aimed this at Jeffrey.

You know why I'm not able to be around as much lately, said Jeffrey, as he clanked his glass against the edge of his plate. We've been over this.

Right. Clod is acting funny, you said.

When she was wound up, Janis called Claudia, Clod.

Well, in case you hadn't noticed, Janis continued, so am I.

Yes, you *are* acting funny, he said. Any more wine?

He stood.

Only champagne.

Champagne?

I was saving it for a special occasion.

Well, here it is, he said.

What?

Our first fight. Where is it?

Fridge, she gestured. Get flutes too.

Jeffrey smiled. Image is everything, isn't it.

He didn't mean to be unkind, thought Janis. And he probably didn't mean to open that can of worms, either.

No, she said. Now that you've mentioned it, image, it turns out, isn't everything.

Explain, he said coming back into the room.

Okay. Dom and I do spend a lot of time together. And yes, he is seen by the neighbours in this building coming in and out of my apartment at all hours, and I'm sure they've remarked on this to you – probably it was Mrs Mifflin – who, by the way, seems to think you're someone I'm trying to discourage since I seem to invite you over so infrequently – and, don't interrupt me please, she said and then realized he was just asking if she wanted a full glass and she nodded yes. And, said Janis as she restarted her rant, and I wear his shirts, mostly because they are more expensive than mine and he likes to iron, and in a lot of ways he is a better companion than you are and there are moments lately when I wish he wasn't gay!

I think you're scaring him.

What are you talking about?

He called me at work.

Dom called you?

Yesterday, said Jeffrey.

He called you?

Yes, he said he was worried about you. He says you're obsessive.

Oh, she laughed, I'm obsessive? This from the guy who for the last week has been singing at the top of his lungs, 'Love, Love, Love'.

So he *is* in love with you.

Try a lawyer named Chase.

Oh.

But wait a minute, said Janis. He called you yesterday. He's never called you before, so obviously he must be concerned or something, and you wait till this evening to see me?

It's not like that.

Sure it is, she said, check your watch. It's eight-thirty. The evening news has finished. It's officially night.

I couldn't get away. Claudia is never home these days and the kids need me.

The kids are fifteen and fourteen. I bet they aren't even home.

But what if they came home? asked Jeffrey.

Or, maybe, what if she came home?

What?

You heard me, said Janis, half a glass stronger. I think you want her to come home, I think you're scared.

Of what?

Why she isn't home. Of him.

Who? said Jeffrey, as if she knew the name of the man he thought his wife was having an affair with.

So, that's how it is, it's okay for you to have someone else, but it's not okay for her?

Why are you being so hard on me?

Why are you being so hard on *me*? said Janis realizing her voice suggested she was about to cry.

Don't cry, she cautioned herself.

Out in the hallway as he was unlocking his door, Domino sang haltingly, 'Hey, Romeo! Rom-eee-oh!'

He opened the door and clanged his keys into a heap on the small table Janis had bought him from the shop.

… 'Romeo?' he sang. He continued humming loudly as he walked deeper into his apartment.

Why doesn't he close his damn door? said Jeffrey.

We often have tea together now.

Oh. And he's waiting for you to go over?

Probably.

You can go.

I know I can go, but thanks for your permission, Janis said and for some reason thought of her mother.

That's not what I meant, Jeffrey said softly, I just don't want to talk about her any more.

'Where the hell are you?' sang Domino.

I'll go tell him, Janis said and kissed Jeffrey.

That night Janis had at least two dreams. The first was dark and grainy. When she reflected on it at work the next morning, she thought it reminded her of documentary footage, like something she might have seen on the news the night before without realizing it. The lighting in the dream was dark. She was inside a high-ceilinged old house, or maybe it was more like a renovated barn. She wasn't sure, but she did know it was a large shop that sold antiques and collectibles and was owned by Claudia, Jeffrey's wife.

Imogene was in the shop with Janis. At times Claudia was there, near the cash register, an antique black thing, other times she wasn't. Janis remembered wandering throughout the store really studying things. She didn't feel nervous about being near Claudia, didn't wonder where Jeffrey was, she was busy looking.

Janis reached high up, towards a basket on the shelf that ran around the room. It was a dark wood, about eight feet from the floor. She was standing on tiptoe, about to lift the top off a milk-painted blue basket, and she was pretty sure she wanted to purchase it, when Jeffrey walked in.

He'd been out buying the Saturday papers before they were all sold out. Before Janis could talk to him, though she didn't really feel compelled to do so, Imogene motioned for her to come over near the antique telephone.

Here, you talk to him, Imogene said.

Who is it?

Benny, of course.

Why *of course?* thought Janis. It was then she noticed the wedding dress her sister was taking out of a large plastic bag. Along with the dress was a roll of gold-sparkled material. As Janis was about to say hello to Benny, she knew or was told that the material had been purchased to make the skirt float more. Imogene planned to sew the material in waves under the white tulle skirt.

Must be something she learned in ballet, thought Janis, thinking for the first time that maybe it really was a more practical pursuit than she'd known. Janis thought about how good the gold would look barely shimmering beneath the white cloud, and how it was only natural that Benny would be on the phone. After all, he and her sister would get married as soon as they graduated from high school that summer.

Benny said hello and said he was working on his math homework.

Then Janis woke up.

As she repositioned the expensive sheets around her, she thought she remembered Claudia and Jeffrey talking briefly in the dream. What were they talking about? she asked her sleepy memory.

The second dream seemed much shorter. And lighter. It was entirely in bright sunlight. The dream seemed to be of an afternoon picnic.

October probably, thought Janis, because there were leaves on the grass and on the paved paths. Early October, she told herself as she dusted the shelves and racks, there were still some red and orange leaves.

She and Jeffrey were sitting on a blanket. Crackers, cheese, smoked oysters, a bottle of wine, two plastic goblets, salami, and something chocolate spread out between them. It seemed perfectly natural to the dream couple that they were having their picnic in a graveyard.

Janis sprayed a mirror and started to wipe. She knew the graveyard, it was the one she passed on the subway twice a day.

That's why it's in the dream, she told her reflection, I see it so often and it's always so lovely. Must cost a million to be buried there, she continued, trying to change the subject her subconscience, as she called it, might be suggesting.

Money, she told the mirror.

Three shoppers and Faye looked at Janis.

Oh, money, I meant to tell you I did the cash already. I got in pretty early this morning.

Couldn't sleep? asked Faye.

Well, I kept having these slightly weird dreams. The last one ended at five, so I thought I might as well get up. See the sunset, all that, said Janis trying to sound light.

You mean sunrise, don't you? And how weird? asked Faye.

Janis could see one of the shoppers would have asked if she hadn't.

Nothing to keep you from going to get us our morning coffee, said Janis. Milk, not cream.

She added, I did the reconciliation for you, shelf under the cash, behind the shoe box, where the deposit bag usually is.

Faye looked sideways at her. You sure are efficient when you're having a crisis. Did it work out?

What?

The cash, the reconciliation sheet, all that?

Oh yeah, no problem, no divorce.

What? said Faye.

Sorry. Reconciliation just seems like a strange word for what we do with the money and charge slips and cheques and sales and laya-ways. Janis took a breath. Was I on a rant again?

I think so, said Faye. I'll get you a dark roast.

So Jeffrey has a conference in Halifax this weekend?

Faye made her reentrance with a cardboard tray of coffees and cinnamon rolls. She handed one to Janis and said, You needed one. Eat.

Janis had been caught off guard. Not by the roll, but by Faye mentioning Jeffrey. She didn't think she'd told her anything – she'd really only told Domino, her sisters and her mother about him, she thought.

Don't sweat it, Faye said as if reading her mind, it was on a pad near the cash. Who's Jeffrey?

Good question, thought Janis as she moved toward the boxes of new stock. A friend, she said slitting tape.

Oh, good, Faye said, new shipment was on the list too, I think. And something about chocolate and eggs maybe?

Janis looked toward the cash.

I threw it out, said Faye. I hope that's okay, it didn't look important.

Thought Janis, It's only my life, as she unfolded the packing slip.

You usually seem more excited about new stuff, said Faye.

I must be tired.

Those fancy sheets don't give you a million-dollar sleep?

Janis blushed and said, No, not really.

I didn't know you had a king-sized bed. Wouldn't that take up a lot of room in an apartment?

Why wouldn't Faye let things drop? wondered Janis as she tried to unpack more loudly and with more deliberateness. But the first thing she pulled out stopped her.

Sleepers?

Hmmmm?

Faye was reading a catalogue that had come in the mail. It looked like a travel catalogue – not much to do with Cash and Clothed Janis knew, but Faye could justify reading anything at work. She spent most of her day reading, going to get change they didn't need, buying supplies they hadn't run out of, picking up coffee, or eating lunch nearby, or 'networking' she said with the other merchants.

If she wasn't so interesting or usually funny, Janis thought she would have resented her more. As it was, Janis felt like she ran the shop but didn't have to be so terrified of all the responsibility because she really didn't have the title.

Image again, thought Janis, once in a while. It can be frightening.

Whereas the image of assistant manager was so much easier, looser, fun without fear, she'd say.

Baby sleepers?

Our new line. What do you think?

We're carrying baby stuff now?

Yeah, isn't it great?

Why am I so upset about this? Janis asked herself and felt her face getting red. She pulled out a stack of tissue-paper-wrapped velour sleepers. They were the colours of the eggs her mother was connected to. And they reminded her of the dream she'd had.

She and her mother were in a large department store. Not unusual. Some of her happiest memories were of going to Toronto with her mother and Imogene and Peggy-Leigh for back-to-school clothes.

Bay Lake has no selection, Iris would say. The quality's not great. If we're going to spend money on clothes, I want them to be good.

Imogene and Peggy-Leigh would groan at this.

Why can't we just dress like everybody else? Peggy-Leigh would say, slouching in the front seat.

I want the sneakers you can get at Towers, said Imogene, Melody's got them.

I want to get you good shoes, Iris would always say, remembered Janis who never quite understood the conversation. She liked whatever her mother picked out for her, and sometimes, when she spotted something herself, her mother would agree readily too. Things seemed fine on those shopping trips. Janis loved the smell of Eaton's, liked being in a change room with her mother while her mother tried on a dress or pantsuit. The girls would always get a lot more than their mother, but usually Iris got one thing, thought Janis as she lifted out more little indoor snowsuits, that's what they reminded her of. She traced the zipper up the little leg to the torso, up to where a chin would be. Babies didn't have necks, did they? Janis wondered and stopped unpacking. There was so much she didn't know about babies. All she did know came from spending too much time watching television while waiting for Jeffrey to call or show up. She was confused about how babies developed. There were gaps, she thought, and suddenly she wanted to know what went on in those spaces of time.

What happens to babies day by day? she asked Faye.

What do you mean? said Faye.

And then Faye also said, What am I saying? I mean, why ask me, I haven't a clue and don't ever want to find out!

In the years Janis had known Faye, Faye never stopped letting people know she was one woman who didn't want kids.

Really, she said, and don't tell me I'll feel differently when I'm older, because I won't.

This was why Janis was so surprised by the latest shipment.

It's an industry, said Faye. Babies.

A woman was holding up the pink sleepers. These are adorable. And so soft. How much?

We haven't priced them yet, said Janis looking down the packing slip. She paused then said, Oh, here they are. Thirty.

The shopper looked at her. Really? That much?

Says so here.

Well they D O feel wonderful.

The shopper continued talking about the sleepers to Janis and Faye but Janis wasn't listening. She was remembering the dream.

She and her mother had been in an Eaton's on one of their long-ago shopping trips. Janis wasn't a child in the dream, but she didn't feel like her present age either. She couldn't tell for sure, but she thought her mother was the age she was supposed to be, around fifty-five.

They were heading for the furniture floor.

Just to see what's new, said Janis's mother.

Janis always thought Iris was being funny then because in a store, wasn't everything new?

Near the escalator, Janis saw Iris pause.

Look at these, she said.

Janis made a face. Aren't those baby clothes?

Yes, look, it's supposed to be a bunny.

Janis was confused. And had a sense that she was dreaming. It was a strange feeling.

When Jeffrey had phoned out of the blue at seven that morning just as she was heading out the door, Janis tried to tell him about her dreams. They didn't get very far. When he called back five minutes later, he said Claudia and a woman friend had come back, having forgotten something for her breakfast meeting.

She's forgetting a lot of things lately, said Jeffrey sounding worried.

Janis was thinking as she picked up a yellow pair of tights, about a foot long. If she'd gotten to this part of the dream, about her feeling like it was a dream and that somehow, weird as it was to be looking at baby clothes with her mother, it was also okay, almost nice, Jeffrey would have probably told her it was postmodern. She thought she'd understood his brief explanation of it to her at that first conference dinner.

She paused. Passion seemed long ago and far away to her. She quietly sang Janis Ian's lyrics.

A bunny, her dream Iris was saying. Look at the terry cloth ears on the hood. And there's even a puff tail, she exclaimed turning them around. We have to get these.

Who for? Janis was remembering the whole dream then, as Faye rang up the pink sleepers for the customer. She asked, Iris, who are they for? I'm too big for those now.

Her mother laughed. I know that, silly. They're for your baby.

And then Janis had woken again.

To be. Or not to be mine.

Janis?

What?

By the way she had spun around as she said this, it was obvious to Domino that Janis hadn't known anyone would hear her.

Nothing, he grinned, I've just never heard you act before.

How long have you been in my apartment? Janis asked as she dropped a stack of new magazines. She picked them up and carried them into the kitchen, dodging the ironing board, which was dividing the rooms. She piled the glossy faces on top of the stove.

Not long, just doing some ironing for you.

And watching 'Courtroom TV'? Janis walked to the television and flicked it off.

Well, maybe just a bit. You know my TV isn't as big as yours, and while we know size isn't everything, well ...

Oh, and you would want to see trials large as life, right?

What's your problem? asked Domino, spraying a shirt. It was one of his shirts that you had to wear cufflinks with. He'd developed a habit of using the key Janis had given him to let himself in when she was at work – he ironed his shirts for her to wear. Sometimes he borrowed back one or two and ironed some of her garment-dyed T-shirts for himself – he liked them under a blazer.

Get some tea, love, he said, and sit on the couch and let it out.

Janis sighed and did as she was told. Do you want to have a child?

Domino looked up and the iron froze an inch above a white shirt. With you, you mean?

No, silly. I mean, do you think about children? Do you think about whether you'd like to have one or two or more and how you will deal with that?

Oooh, Domino exhaled. He put the iron down as if he was practising having just watched for the first time someone else do it. Where do you get some of these big questions and why don't you give some kind of sign first, like a turn signal?

Sorry, and you don't have to talk about this if you'd rather not, it's just …

Her voice trailed into the sound of swallowing tea.

It's just what? asked Domino.

I don't know. I'm thinking a lot these days about a baby.

Any baby in particular?

Well, mine. I mean mine and Jeffrey's.

Oh, my God, said Domino, spilling tea on the T-shirt he'd borrowed from Janis.

She watched the colour turn darker where the liquid fell. He looked delighted.

No, she stopped him, I'm not pregnant.

His face fell as he said, Then I don't get it.

I want to be. I really want to have a baby.

Wow. You're about as serious as I've ever heard you except when you're rhapsodizing about thread-counts and percale this and London Fog that.

Janis grinned and sank into the couch a bit. Why hadn't she talked to Domino about this before? she wondered. What about you?

You mean kids?

Janis nodded carefully. She was afraid she'd somehow jinx Domino's words if they were about to come out.

He held his mug in both hands. Sure, I think about it. I'm thirty-three, you know, the old biological tick, tick.

I thought only women had that?

Well, maybe. Anyway, mine feels more like a tick, you know, the kind that buries itself beneath your skin.

He sighed while trying to laugh and coughed as a result.

I want kids, Domino continued. I really don't know many people who don't. And sometimes I talk about it with, you know, whomever I'm with.

Like Chase?

Not yet. Not long enough. And I can't read him. Some guys it's easy to tell.

Domino held up her pink T-shirt against his chest.

Sometimes, he said, they mention it first. I was in love once with a guy who was divorced and had custody of his daughter. It took me a year to figure out I loved him because he had a kid.

Janis squeezed his hand. I figured you'd want kids. I just never thought to talk to you about it until now.

She put her mug down on the blanket box and wanted to say something more, anything.

But you'd make a great dad. Then she blushed. Or mom.

Thanks, dear, he said patting her knee. They'd know all the words to Broadway shows.

Don't change this channel we're on, she said, I'm still watching. About this child thing. Maybe it was the new shipment – I know I've been thinking about kids the last two years, I just didn't have to admit it before, or didn't want to.

You see them everywhere, right? said Domino.

You too?

Domino nodded.

I'm sure there've always been as many strollers and carriages and backpacks, said Janis. But I really notice them now. It's all I can do not to touch their little heads or feel their mini hands sticking out of a pouch some woman or man is carrying. I'm afraid I will. I'm pathetic.

You need more tea, said Domino, getting up. I'll start more water, stay still.

You'll make someone a fine spouse, Janis called above the noise of the kitchen tap.

I know, sang Domino. Want toast with that?

Yes.

Maybe I just need some food, said Janis, maybe that's all this is, low blood sugar.

Don't go denying this, now, Domino said, plopping down on the couch right beside Janis.

He put his arm around her and gave her a friendly squeeze. Then he lifted his legs and crossed them on top of hers.

Have we told the beloved yet?

What do you think? And don't call him that, said Janis.

Oh, guess not. Are we planning on telling him?

I was. Several times this week actually, and last. But he's a bit preoccupied.

With what? His books? The ivory tower? The wife?

Yes, her. The Clod.

She might not want you to have his child, Domino said.

Janis tended to clam up when things got real. She knew this about herself and was grateful for her ability to flee. She imagined she was fishing with her father. She'd told Domino about those times. Janis said talking to her father on those fishing evenings or early mornings was almost better than getting a fish. And she'd try to stay still, she said, not so as not to scare the fish away, but so that her father would, as he always did, start to relax and to get kind of introspective for him, and he'd begin to talk about work, or what he wanted to do to fix up the cabin. Sometimes he'd talk about Iris. Or Imogene or Peggy-Leigh whom they'd caught smoking and skipping school.

Best, said Janis, was when he talked about his parents and about fishing with his father, or picking peaches with his mother and sisters, or about the farm they had once and the animals.

My father fixed up old houses, he'd said one morning when they were in the aluminum boat, and then we'd sell them. We always moved just when the house was nice. But it was always interesting, getting them when no one else thought they'd be saved. It was like proving my father was right all along. Even my mother thought he was crazy a few times.

Domino continued. Really, what *about* Claudia?

Yes, well, Janis thought she sounded close to tears and it surprised her, I don't know. I thought they were finished. When I met Jeffrey I didn't think he wanted her to stay. Now, I don't know.

Her voice trailed off faraway. She imagined a rowboat rowing on a calm evening lake. It rowed around the point and seemed gone. Have you talked to Jeffrey? he asked.

About her or about kids?

Either or both.

Yes, both. Usually not together, or maybe together. I don't know any more. We seem to have hit a snag.

Maybe time to cut the line and start the motor?

What? said Janis.

Sorry, said Domino quickly, just a bad fishing analogy.

I think that's really what I need, Janis said evenly.

A bad analogy?

No, fishing. I've been thinking I want to go home this weekend. See Iris and Dad. Want to come?

No, thanks. Chase has promised to watch me cook.

Sounds fun. And kinky, said Janis.

I hope so. It *is* a holiday weekend. What about your lover?

Halifax, said Janis. A conference all three days – he says I'd be bored stiff, he'd be in workshops the whole time.

She looked at the teapot. I guess he's right. And he was kind of sweet the way he said he would have taken me, but that he knows how I hate to fly and wouldn't want to put me through that if he couldn't even spend the days with me.

There are nights, aren't there? said Domino.

Yes, but he would be tired. Janis stopped. I sound like I'm making excuses, don't I?

No, it sounds like he is.

You don't like him, do you? said Janis narrowing her eyes.

Honestly?

Janis nodded.

No.

You used to, didn't you?

Maybe. What is the correct answer? he asked.

She shrugged.

Why do you hate flying? he asked. Is this a sexual thing?

No, very funny. Janis was grateful for the change of pace. It's because in grade two Melody Hansen's father died when his plane crashed into a cloud.

You're kidding?

No. That's what they told her and that's what she told us at recess. Janis got up and carried the cups into the kitchen.

Wow, at least a small fortune in therapy there. Want to borrow mine? asked Domino.

Your shrink?

Yes, I think he can fit you in the two days a week I don't see him.

Janis laughed. No, not yet. But if I can't handle this baby thing, I'll let you know.

Make sure. I get a discount if I supply enough new patients, you know, it's like a record club.

It is *not*, said Janis. Is it?

It turned out that Janis couldn't go home Thanksgiving weekend. At the last minute, Thursday night to be exact, Faye called to ask could she, Janis, work Saturday after all?

Janis was surprised by how forcefully her *no* came out. You know I've got a seat on the bus already, I'm supposed to leave right after work tomorrow, remember?

It's only Bay Lake, it's not like it's not gonna be there next weekend, or forever after.

It's Thanksgiving, remember? said Janis.

You're not religious.

Neither are you, said Janis. You still haven't said why you suddenly can't work. And it is your turn for Saturday.

Actually, they were supposed to alternate Saturdays. They never did. Janis couldn't remember the last time she had a Saturday off. It must have been the last time she had gone to see her parents.

Bruce wants to go camping.

Cold for that, no? Janis asked. She knew she was referring to her boss, not to the weather.

Oh, I know, said Faye. And I think I can convince him to check into this nice bed and breakfast I know about in cottage country once we get there and he realizes it feels like snow. There's been frost every night! Men!

This, Janis realized, was meant to draw her into the conspiracy. Aren't men jerks? And aren't we smart for knowing it? These were the messages Janis thought Faye was counting on. Then Janis would relent.

Faye obviously picked up on my problematic love life, she thought.

Janis considered relenting – really, she wasn't giving up a weekend at a romantic bed and breakfast, fireplaces, walks through leaves, a cold paddle in a canoe, fireplaces, fireplaces, fireplaces for two. She was obsessed she realized, and her boss was still on the phone waiting for an answer.

I am a warehouse waiting to be filled, said Janis.

What was that? asked Faye.

Receiving blankets, thought Janis. Ivory, pink, blue, or a mix. All cotton. Hand-woven. And even diaper bags.

Yesterday she felt she had to have a diaper bag. What would she do with it? Not to mention the Snugli, which had made her cry when she hung it up.

You okay? Faye had asked as she breezed out for another break. Allergies, said Janis. And after Faye had gone, Janis added, I'm allergic to my life as it is.

Sure.

Sure what? asked Faye.

Sure, I'll work. Maybe I'll still go north on Saturday night. That's the spirit, said Faye.

You're welcome. Janis realized she was pushing it but couldn't stop herself.

Thank you, of course. But, added Faye, these are the privileges of being a manager. Some day you too can do this.

Be a shit? thought Janis. I don't think so.

Whatever, Janis said.

No, Janis thought, she didn't understand her parents. When she'd called to say she had to work and to ask, should she come later, her father said, No.

No?

We'll come down. You always visit us and spend your money getting here, Mother and I can make the trip.

Really?

It'll do us good to get to the big city.

He always called it that. And compared to Bay Lake it was. Janis was starting to think it could be fun to have her parents stay with her for the holiday.

What about Imogene?

She's busy with something, Ray said. Oh, your mother wants to talk.

Iris got on the phone. I'll tell you about Imogene later. Your father doesn't know.

About Benny?

The baby.

What baby?

Can't talk now, sweetie.

Then, Janis noticed, her mother added, It's too expensive, loud enough for Ray to hear.

He was probably watching football anyway.

I heard your father say we were going to your place, it sounds like a lovely idea.

Are you two okay?

Feel fine. Your father has a cold but it's almost gone.

And before Janis could interrupt she said, Well, I'll go pack a few things and we shouldn't spend all your money on the phone. See you soon.

What baby?

Bye, sweetie.

Janis was still wondering what was going on in Bay Lake when she got to work the next morning. Friday mornings were often quiet. She'd been thinking most of the night, she couldn't tell if she'd slept until she remembered a dream. The security guy had helped her unlock the door – he held her coffee – and he looked just like the man in her dream.

The man of my dream, she laughed to herself as she turned on the lights.

The little pot lights shone down like stars in the cedar ceiling sky. These days she liked the store best when she was in without Faye. The work wasn't any more than if the official manager had been in. Janis was beginning to realize she'd been managing ever since she was hired. In the last week, managing had suddenly become something she didn't want.

I don't want to manage, she'd told herself on the subway home at night, or as she sat through all the channels in search of something more and wanting Jeffrey to call.

Yes, I can manage, she'd say, but do I want to? I want to do more than manage.

The man in her dream hadn't been alone. It figures, she thought ruefully as she counted the float on Friday. She'd closed the night before, so she knew the money would be accurate, but she was in the habit of counting since Faye frequently screwed up.

The man had arrived with a woman and another man. They were standing at her door when she opened it. The door was her front door – in the dream she owned a large white farm house.

Opening the door, she saw the three strangers and the lake behind them. Before the lake there was her large sloping front lawn, then the road, and then lots of brush, which edged the lake.

Janis couldn't remember exact dialogue from her dream, but while looking in one of the new mirrors in the store, she remembered the people were landscapers who wanted to know if, now that she'd moved in, she wanted to fix up the yard. The strangers said they could plant trees for her. One of the men, the one who looked like the security guard, said she should let him plant and clear-out the brush area before it's too late. Too late? For what? she'd asked.

He smiled. He said the land was already growing over, and already she'd lost some of her property forever, but he could help her save what was left.

She believed him and in the dream was ready to say yes. But just then she said, I'm sure you're right. And I think I want you to do what you've said, but, and in daylight the words sounded even stranger than they'd felt in the dream, I'll have to check with my husband.

What husband? Even in the dream she'd quietly wondered, did she have one?

I must have, she thought, or I wouldn't have said that.

The woman in the dream had smiled at her then. Or grinned? Janis wasn't sure. And the other man just stood around. She never saw his face.

This must be a new mirror, thought Janis, I look different.

She moved her bangs one way and then the other. She did look different, but she couldn't decide why. Maybe it was because she was wearing gloves. Indoors. She'd found the blue gloves on the floor near the cash register. The gloves had small beads around the cuffs. Very elegant. Very lovely. So lovely, she'd bought them a year ago for her mother for Christmas.

How did they get here? Janis asked the mirror. It's not even that cold out. And where is my mother? Did she break in?

Janis tilted her head on her gloved hands as if she were a movie star and gazed into the mirror. Wonder what this one's supposed to do, she said, then turned to see if any customers had snuck in and heard her. You were never supposed to mention that the mirrors did special tricks. The Bible said. You could get fired for less.

She tried to imagine what Imogene would look like pregnant.

Probably like I would look, thought Janis, if that ever happens. She took off the gloves and picked up a cushion. Then a hand-knit blue cardigan. It was a large and just fit when she put it on and then tucked the cushion under it.

Imogene is a bit smaller than me, she thought, but our features are pretty much the same. I guess she'll look like this.

And then she thought of Russ. As far as Janis knew, Russ hadn't been home in half a year. He was living in less than basic conditions way up north. Imogene wasn't expected to visit him up there, by Russ or anyone, it was that cold and that lacking in facilities like indoor plumbing.

So the baby must not be his, thought Janis, it's Benny. And then she smiled, A little Benny. What would they do? Imogene and Benny, Russ and Martha. Martha had always been hard to figure out when they were all together in high school. A nice girl, but always working at her father's bait business and always smelling vaguely of fish. People had heard Benny and Martha were having problems, Willow Junction was a small place, but this would certainly top their list of difficulties, no doubt.

At least Martha has her own income, thought Janis, it could be worse. She's worked her way up at Goodmart, that's something.

She was still looking at her stomach in the mirror when she heard two voices at the front of the store, near the Oriental rug. It was hanging on the wall in such a way that it drew people, who otherwise would have walked past the store, into Cash and Clothed.

This is perfect, said one woman.

The other said, It *is* lovely.

It's the right colours and everything. See the blue? It's the same as the walls in the livingroom. And I think the couch that's there would go okay. Wow, I really think this might work! Janis decided to listen in a little longer before she went over.

It would cover that mess, you know where I mean?

The other woman nodded.

I mean, no one would ever know anything had happened there. And the fireplace, well, it draws your attention away.

You're probably right, said the other woman.

It would look like a normal fireplace, like nothing had happened.

Has anyone looked at the house?

No, said the woman, whom Janis had decided to dislike. The woman who'd spotted the rug first. The woman seemed to have a ruthless quality, and seemed to be hiding something.

No one. Not even a nibble. You'd think people would at least be curious. You know, want to see the damage. Look for marks, or something. Frankly, I'm surprised. How much is this? she yelled in Janis's direction without pausing to breathe.

Janis hated being yelled at. She slowly walked over and was almost close to the two women when the other one smiled and asked, When?

Pardon?

Your baby? You're walking like the weight is really something now.

Janis blushed and panicked and then thought, Hey, if they think I am, I am. January, she blurted, hoping that worked numerically.

Your first?

Oh, yes. And the rug, let's see, Janis said, leaning a little to reach the tag.

Oh, I can check, said the nice woman. Here. Claudia, it's fifteen-hundred.

Janis felt the cushion move suddenly. It was as if she'd been kicked, not hard, almost like she imagined a baby kick would feel, but she'd definitely been kicked. The mean woman's name was Claudia, and she'd said she sold real estate.

Excuse me, she said, be right back.

She went over to the phone, as if she had an important call to a shipper that she had to make. Flipping through the yellow pages, she tried to listen to Claudia.

The open house is this weekend. It's got to work.

Sunday?

Yes. And then she laughed. And can you believe it? Jeffrey thought we should go away this weekend!

The other woman didn't say anything to this, just had a strange look on her face.

Probably not unlike how I look right now, thought Janis as she looked toward a mirror.

She wanted to take the cushion out, but realized it was too late now. She wanted to stop listening in, but realized that too was no longer an option.

That's what I thought, said Claudia to the other woman. Why would Jeffrey and I go away?

Where? the nice woman finally said quietly.

Oh, don't get upset, I didn't go with him, did I? And she squeezed the woman's arm in the first hint of warmth Janis had seen.

Then Claudia leaned closer to the woman. In a lowered voice she said, I told you it's been over for years. We only stayed together for the kids.

Janis couldn't breathe. She checked in a mirror to see if she was gasping as much as she thought she was. What she saw startled her.

It wasn't her stress which struck her, it was a shiny pink dot in the reflection. On one of the shelves across the store, there appeared to be a foil egg.

On the next shelf down there was a purple one.

A blue one was lower down.

And the money, Claudia added louder. You know we couldn't put our house back on the market right away, it wouldn't sell. And then the market fell out, and well, you know.

The other woman was looking at Claudia.

Don't spoil our day, Chris. Remember? He's gone. He went anyway, last night. He's in Halifax by now, although God knows what he's going to do with himself for three days. Doesn't know anyone there. Hasn't even got a conference! Can you believe he bought this package deal – airfare, hotel, meals, the tall ships, the whole bit without asking me?

Chris, Janis noticed, still wasn't saying much.

I know why he didn't ask me, continued Claudia, her voice rising, it's because he knew I'd say no. How ridiculous! What was he thinking?

Chris finally spoke. What *was* he thinking? And *why* would he think it?

Janis thought Claudia looked a bit surprised. Near the cash register, Janis sat down heavily on a stool. The stool the Bible said not to sit on as it sent the wrong message. But why have it there? Janis often thought. She counted eggs around the room.

Maybe this is why it's here, she said.

The women looked at her and then they both looked as if they were hearing things. They resumed their conversation.

Okay, so he WAS thinking there was a chance of a reconciliation, Claudia admitted. But I don't know why? We've hardly seen each other in months, it's been great actually.

What about Sunday mornings?

What *about* Sunday mornings? Janis wanted to scream.

I told you, said Claudia as she took Chris by the arm, that's over. We haven't made love in a year.

Janis couldn't hear what Chris said to that because in her mind she was yelling, A year? Only a year? I've been with Jeffrey longer than that, what's going on?

She was sure he'd said they hadn't really had sex since Ivy was conceived. Maybe that had been a bit optimistic, Janis thought.

A year? said Chris.

I *told* you, said Claudia trying to quiet her, sometimes I *had* to on Sunday mornings. Or he'd be awful with the kids. I was afraid he'd upset them and tell them we were planning to separate and it didn't make sense to tell them when we couldn't do it right away, don't you see?

Janis did see. But she didn't know what Chris saw. Could everyone see the eggs? She didn't really care. She dialled Domino's number only briefly wondering if she'd be interrupting a morning with Chase.

She's here, she said when Domino sleepily answered.

Who? And who is this?

You know it's me. I'm at the store. Clod the sod is here.

Wow, said Domino fully awake. You're sure?

Positive. And I know where Clod trod.

She glanced over at the two women who were lifting the rug off its wall hooks. She should have helped but she was beyond caring about the store, the rug, Jeffrey, all that.

He lied to me.

About what? Can you talk, is she close?

I can talk now, I'll let you know if she comes closer.

Janis grabbed her breath and started in a rush. He lied about Halifax and Sunday mornings and my fear of flying and everything! Like how he wants her back!

Should I come down?

Domino's concern snapped Janis out of it a bit. Isn't Chase there?

Right beside me, want to say hi? He's awake now too.

Sorry. No. I really am sorry.

Domino interrupted her. Don't be, I'm teasing. And I *will* come down if you want.

Yes, I was calling about some flower arrangements for our *anniversary* sale next week?

What? said Domino.

Janis said slowly, Maybe two or three, something simple that suggests fall and anniversaries, that kind of thing.

Then in a quieter voice, She's coming over, let's try something. I'd like some *ivy* in them. She said ivy louder than the rest. Claudia looked up. She stopped talking for a moment and then resumed touching the carpet which she and Chris had draped over two wicker chairs.

I get it, said Domino. Did she hear?

Yes, my mother carried some in her *wedding* bouquet thirty-five years ago. She planted it after and I have the plant in my apartment now, the stuff lasts longer than *some marriages*, she said.

No response.

Louder Janis said, *Ivy sure is amazing.*

Claudia looked at her.

Oh, you can't fit us in next week because you're doing something for an *Ivy-League* college?

Better stop it, said Domino sounding serious for once.

Why? asked Janis twisting the phone cord.

Are you sure you want to blow it with Jeffrey?

It's blown, said Janis, and then added, *Our budget's* pretty well blown for promotions, in case Claudia was really listening. *So really anything quick and simple and appropriate would work.* And then she couldn't resist saying, How about *poison ivy.*

At that Claudia walked over to the cash. She was looking extremely agitated.

I'm dead, thought Janis, feeling like maybe this was a not-bad thing. As Claudia leaned towards her Janis suddenly remembered another dream.

She was in a kitchen. Four men were seated around a breakfast table. They'd made eggs for her. Apparently they all could cook. And they all were divorced. And they all were nice. One was Russ. These guys aren't so bad, Janis remembered thinking in the dream. And remembered asking, Why didn't I think they were out there?

Get off the phone, said Claudia.

Well, thanks for your time, said Janis, please call back *soon* with your estimate.

I estimate she's pissed off, said Domino.

Thanks again and bye-bye, said Janis.

We want this rug and we are double-parked. I assumed you could finish your call when you didn't have a big sale waiting.

Chris was holding up the rug like a big torch and looking apologetic.

Janis was thinking, How can you love *her*? And then answered herself, Well, Jeffrey might have at first. And, she had to admit, I love Jeffrey.

She'd meant to think *loved*, past tense.

I'm not sure it will go, Claudia said.

Janis knew she was lying.

And the size might be all wrong.

Janis said, Size isn't everything, and I think you know what I'm talking about.

Claudia did not acknowledge Janis's wink.

Janis could see what was going on. After the open house, after prospective home-buyers had walked on the rug, Claudia would be back saying how sad she was that it just wouldn't work with her decor.

But Janis realized she really didn't care. Would you like that gift-wrapped? she asked. And I can throw in a few Easter eggs.

* * *

While they were having coffee the next morning, Janis said to her mother, I like the idea of team-building.

Her mother reached over the table and pulled the blinds all the way up as she said, I thought you hated that conference.

I did. I'm not talking about work, I'm talking about the rest of my life. And, Janis added, her eyes widening, I think you know what I'm talking about.

Do I?

Come on, Mom. Dad's going to be back soon and you know he won't want to talk about these sorts of things, he doesn't even seem to like to listen to them, does he?

Iris sighed. Your father thinks about just this kind of thing, family is very important to him, it's taken me thirty-five years to figure out that's why he won't talk.

She poured more coffee for Janis and herself. Of course, you should cut down.

Cut down?

On caffeine. I read that it can interfere with conception.

Janis missed her mouth by the smallest of fractions and caught a drip of coffee sliding down her chin. Maybe Dad just needs you to talk about things more slowly, less directly. Then she ventured, Is that why you've been leaving eggs?

What?

Janis wondered if her mother really wasn't conscious of her behaviour, or whether the eggs had appeared some other way.

Maybe, she thought, there never were any eggs, maybe I just wanted there to be.

Why do you think he brought your old fishing pole?

Good question, laughed Janis. It's not like I can fish anywhere around here.

He thought you might need some things that reminded you of home, of family, of where you came from.

Is he trying to tell me something?

He knows about Jeffrey, said Iris, lowering her cup.

Knows what about Jeffrey? said Janis wondering how much to tell her mother about the latest Jeffrey. The Jeffrey Janis had really only known about since his wife and her lover dropped into the store for the loan of an expensive carpet.

Why stop here? Janis had wanted to say as Claudia was walking out of the store carrying the rug like a log with Chris on the other end.

It looks more like a dead body. There goes my relationship, thought Janis. Carry the corpse out. Why not go all the way? Why not furnish the house in absolutely the very best – lighting fixtures,

Scotland lace for the windows, how about some dancing cherubs to complete the effect?

The graceful statuette would look wonderful on the mantel in the very room Claudia was so concerned with.

Must have been a crime of passion, thought Janis, with new insight into how those things could occur.

That he's married, said Iris. And that he's not in any rush to change that. Her left eyebrow lifted, which suggested to Janis that she was guessing at this last point.

True, Janis said.

Her mother took her hand. Janis felt about nine years old. Besides, she said, you can hang it on your wall.

Janis was confused. Hang *what* on my wall?

The fishing rod. I've seen it in magazines and it would go well with your hats and baskets, look.

Janis could see her mother was right, not just about the rod, as usual. I remember when he got it for me.

She stared at the rod standing near the sink where her father had put it when they arrived the night before. There was a green button you clicked to let the line out. Janis had an overwhelming urge to let it fly, everything, just fling behind her and then over and out in an arc which would leave her free to stand and watch the silver sinker descend into whatever was beneath. The lake had never looked so clear. Driftwood wasn't just an outline any more, she could see the grain, the gnarled shape of it. How did we get here? she wondered and looked back at her father near the motor. He'd already cast and was waiting, patient as always. She hoped there would be another story, a way into his past and future, along with the fish.

He's right, and so are you, said Janis. Then she said, Mom, I wasn't named after Janis Ian, was I?

Iris looked at her and said nothing. Then she looked at the door. Was that your father buzzing to get into the front entrance?

No. You know he'll be gone at least another few minutes. He likes to explore the big city, as he says. He's probably buying fruit from a stand and thinking about opening one in Bay Lake.

Iris smiled, You're right.

About what? Janis held her breath but tried to look unfazed.

About your name.

Janis moved her chair close. It was Joplin, wasn't it?

Yes, said Iris exhaling.

Why didn't you tell me the truth?

How did you know?

I asked first, said Janis.

I don't know, said Iris.

Janis saw her mother look afraid or embarrassed but she kept trying to talk.

Janis Joplin seemed like a lot to burden a little girl with.

And Janis Ian didn't? Janis laughed.

Well, yes, I see your point, said Iris. It was both, really. Both women.

I know, or I think I know why Janis Ian. But what about Joplin?

That song, I don't even know what it's called, the one that's about the Lord and a Mercedes Benz.

Really? Janis laughed.

Iris smiled. I wanted your middle name to be Mercedes, but your father thought it too strange.

Marie *is* safer, Janis agreed. Janis Mercedes, she said, I like it.

I wanted you to have it all, said Iris staring right at her youngest daughter.

Don't come back right now, Janis silently told her father who would be walking towards the apartment. Stop in the park across the street.

Have what? Janis asked quietly.

Oh, the usual, said Iris, I'm not that original. Feminism made me a cliché, I think, but I wanted you to grow up to be independent – financially and otherwise. I wanted you to have a career and a family. I wanted you to feel just as real outside the home as in it. I wanted you never to have to ask your husband for money, or to wonder how you and your children would manage without him.

Janis was about to say something but her mother lifted her hand as if trying to block a wave from hitting a sand sculpture. Wait, she said. I also wanted you to be as in love with someone as I was with your father.

I still am, she added when she saw Janis's look. I just wanted more. For each of you. And you, you, she said, picking up Janis's mug and putting it in the sink, could have a career and love and family. You wouldn't have to make a choice. Of course, you could if you wanted. Imogene will probably give up instructing for a while, I mean, she'll have to certainly for a bit. And I think she wants to. And Peggy-Leigh seems okay for now at home with her artwork. I gave you my eye for beautiful things, I think, said Iris almost apologizing, and I wanted you to be able to get them. I used to hum Janis Joplin's song when I was pregnant with you and Peggy-Leigh and Imogene were so small and I was probably younger than you are now.

She smiled from where she stood near the sink. I sound crazy, don't I?

No. Janis wanted to say more so she added, And I like her voice, not to mention that hair.

Iris smiled sheepishly. How long have you known?

Only about a week, a magazine had an article about Janis Ian. The dates didn't add up. That's why I thought I'd go home this weekend.

Because you found out the truth?

Well, said Janis, that and a few other things. She gestured towards the wicker bassinet she'd hastily stuck two plants in.

She thought of the packet of birth control pills in her dresser which she wouldn't start taking in a day or two, and how different from Jeffrey the next man she slept with would be.

The Whole Truth

•

Peggy-Leigh had a sixth sense. Always. She just knew things were going to happen before they occurred, and so was rarely surprised after. A gift some would say. Others, a curse.

One of the first was the fire. But who could blame everyone, she thought, for not believing her that time. After all, she had always been scared of fire and maybe they thought she was that boy in the story her mother read to her long ago. Iris was always reading to the three girls, or to herself. That boy who cried, what was it, wondered Peggy-Leigh trying to remember, wolf? Four letters, one syllable, she could see why they caught the similarity and decided not to listen.

We knew it was going to storm, she told Ted on their first date. Ted Whitton was her humanities professor. She was eighteen, in first year general arts, and was attending the ugliest university she could imagine.

Peggy-Leigh had read an article the summer before, while sitting on the new back deck and inhaling the smell of warm cedar, from one of her mother's millions of magazines. It was written in first-person and was titled 'I Am the Teacher's Pet'. It was about a first-year student who was sleeping with her professor. Peggy-Leigh just knew she could end up doing the same. The title of the article reminded her of reading old *Reader's Digests*. 'I Am Joe's Appendix' it would say.

She remembered in particular a story about a guy having meningitis, and about how they'd done a spinal tap on him. She must have only been ten or eleven when she'd read the issue at the cabin.

And at fifteen, her first summer to go to camp, she missed the opening week by becoming very ill. Red dots and a high fever. When her mother, Iris, took her to emergency, a doctor Peggy-Leigh didn't know looked very serious and said above her sweating body, We'd better do a lumbar puncture.

Peggy-Leigh had looked him in the eye and said, A spinal tap?

The doctor looked at her mother.

It might be the measles, Iris said to the doctor, right?

No, said Peggy-Leigh quite evenly. He thinks I might have meningitis.

The doctor and her mother looked at each other. Then at Peggy-Leigh who said, Let's hope the fluid is clear, having read that cloudy was bad.

And so they had done the procedure after wheeling her into a room called the Trauma Room. The name didn't make Peggy-Leigh too relaxed, but she wanted her mother to calm down.

This, she'd recently decided, was her new role in life – since her two younger sisters seemed to require enormous amounts of their mother's energy and attention. Peggy-Leigh decided she should require less, to balance things out. She was the oldest and for years had grown accustomed to stepping aside in favour of Janis and Imogene.

She used to resent it, hate it, like the day it snowed too much and the school closed and their father, Ray, had somehow gotten someone else to drive his plough and to do the run so that he could arrive at the school at two, and be in the schoolyard as they got out. He was near the bicycle rack where in grade two Peggy-Leigh had once smashed her head. A warm day, she'd leaned back, lost her balance and had hit her head on the pavement. Things smelled funny then and her ears felt loose. Her mother had to keep her awake all that afternoon and into the night. It seemed to Peggy-Leigh that she hadn't had her mother to herself like that in years.

Anyway, he was there near the racks, waiting to walk them home down the middle of the street, the snow was that high and there were no cars. She reached for one of the gloved hands he held out but realized, with only two, he had to give them to the younger girls. She shoved hers in the pockets of her purple ski jacket. She hated purple.

So in the hospital that summer day she faked as best she could. As she said bye to her mother at the door, she said, Don't worry. It'll be clear. And then I have to lie without moving *anything* for twenty-four hours, that's all. *Reader's Digest* mentioned a horrible headache otherwise, she added, as the wheels moved and the doors swung shut.

Two nurses held her still. The doctor never once laughed at her jokes which she'd stopped telling as soon as the pain hit. She could feel liquid running down her back, it was the weirdest sensation, she thought, like I'm peeing myself through my back.

She imagined the liquid coming from her brain and wondered what she was losing. Words? Memories? Like before Imogene and Janis had come when there were just her parents. What if these memories left and never came back? What remembrances would she miss the most?

When we left the cabin after dinner and headed into Aunt Ed and Uncle Keith's trailer to play cards, she told Ted, who had said, Call me Ted, when he'd phoned her in her dorm room to ask if she wanted to have pizza on campus and to talk about her paper, it was already raining. The radio had said severe thunder, said Peggy-Leigh sniffing the pizza smells around and remembering she hadn't eaten all day.

She continued her story.

Was there any other kind of thunder? I thought. But for at least a couple of hours we just had Niagara Falls on the roof, but no bang.

Ted Whitton, her fortyish professor, was staring at her. At *me*, she thought, and not at one of the three giggly girls who sat in the row in front of her in the five-hundred-seat lecture theatre. The three drove her nuts. Their hairspray made her dizzy as they tossed their permed, long snakes back in her direction.

She'd only recently cut her hair. Well, shaved was more the word, she thought as she felt the side of her head. She hadn't done it, Guido, of Guido's Barbershop, had done it. Peggy-Leigh had had enough of trying to look like Imogene, the ballerina, the feminine version of herself. She felt her newly naked ear. Seven earrings, little silver stars all of them. She saw Ted counting over the top of his menu. His lips moved.

And then it hit, Peggy-Leigh told him as she slammed her hand on the plastic table between them. Crashes you could feel. I wanted to be anywhere where there wasn't a window. And in the trailer, there were windows everywhere. Everybody turned and looked at me after one particularly big noise. I was sure a tree had been hit, or worse. I started to cry. Again, no one expected less, and someone kept shuffling. I can't remember what we were playing, but I know I wasn't winning.

Ted smiled at her and she thought, Hey, maybe I won *him*!

I never won at cards. It could have been because my sister, Imogene, always cheated. Not on purpose, maybe, but she did. Anyway, my father took one look at me and said, Is that it, kid?

Yep, I said. Let's go.

Would it be all right if I ordered for us? asked Ted, touching her hand.

This silenced her. She thought, Great, I don't have to worry about what to eat, or not eat, this isn't my decision.

And she was grateful. She had an eating disorder. Had for years and she was finally getting good at it, she thought. And so really, the only way she could eat lately had been when other people told her when and what. Then it wasn't her fault, she reasoned.

She nodded at Ted and said, I pretty much like everything.

Except anchovies? he asked.

She knew it was a test. No, I like those too, she said having never tasted them.

He smiled, which told her that she had passed. Peggy-Leigh went back to talking about the long-ago night.

My father and I had this deal, because this happened a few times every summer since I could remember, that I'd hang out with everyone and pretend things were okay, until I couldn't stand it any more, until the storm felt too close. Then he'd swoop me into his arms and race me into the cabin.

Peggy-Leigh waved her arms to demonstrate the swoop. She knocked her menu onto the floor. Ted picked it up for her and she blushed.

Sometimes we ran up from the beach, sometimes back from the woods, down from the cliff, or, as we did this time, in from the trailer. The trailer which always smelled like a trailer even if the windows were never closed.

Ted nodded as if he knew. But Peggy-Leigh was fairly certain the distinguished man across from her had never stepped inside a trailer.

Once inside, I'd crawl into bed. My dad would pull the blind, kiss me, and say, You're okay, as he closed the door.

Peggy-Leigh carefully arranged the remaining bits of pizza crust on her plate.

Then I couldn't see anything much, except for the occasional flash. And then I'd close my eyes and this would work until the thunder and lightning hit so hard, the fuse box would rattle. There would be this metal hum, and I'd imagine my intestines clanging together to make that noise.

Ted raised his eyebrows and Peggy-Leigh wondered if she sounded stupid. How could she not? she thought. She was from Willow Junction. Ted lived in Toronto, drove a sports car which she'd seen parked outside his office building. There were expensive paper shopping bags in the car, from Harry Rosen, and Holt Renfrew. Who was Holt? she wanted to know. But knew she wouldn't ask Ted, ever, if he ever talked to her. And then he had. Just a week ago.

After the lecture on Virginia Woolf, he'd walked from the front of the big theatre over to where she sat.

He's going to tell me I'm too dumb for this course, she thought, and that I have to leave and that I only got my scholarship because Mr Elliott liked kissing me when we were supposed to be working on the yearbook.

But Professor Ted Whitton had chewed out the girls in front of her. If you want to giggle and talk, get out! he said. This young woman behind you is trying to listen to my lecture, she obviously appreciates literature.

The three Medusas turned and stared at Peggy-Leigh. At her shaved head.

She felt she had to say something, to prove that she had been listening for the previous two hours. She said, The stones in her pocket part really moved me. My sisters and I tried it once at the cabin to see if we'd sink.

By then I would be really crying, said Peggy-Leigh, as Ted expertly lifted a piece of pizza onto her plate.

He is taking care of me, she thought, I like this.

I'd be crying, she said again to Ted. But I'd be trying not to let anyone hear, like Imogene who was younger and should have been more scared than me. Janis was too young to know anything. She'd actually watch storms from the big window by the plaid couch. Sometimes I'd get afraid that the lightning would come through the window, hit her, and her head would blow up. But by that point I'd be crying too hard and couldn't make sense enough for my mom or anyone to get Janis away from the window. They'd cart me away into the bedroom when it was Janis they should have been saving.

Ted poured her a glass of red wine, which she hadn't heard him order.

Once, Peggy-Leigh said after a gulp of wine, when Imogene was talking to Benny on the phone, when we finally got one for the cabin, there was a bang which I heard all the way from the bedroom. Imogene screamed and I started wailing and Janis, who was in the bedroom with me and my mother, turned on the light and stared at me. Then she started to cry. My mother ran to the next room and ran into Imogene who was running towards us. The phone had been hit.

It flew out of my hand, Imogene said. I think she was thrilled by it all, Peggy-Leigh added. And from under my pillow, I thought to myself, I knew it.

Ted smiled.

But I knew that everyone always thought I was overreacting.

Peggy-Leigh picked off a pepperoni slice and sucked on it as she said, Although there was a brief period, after the fire, when I did have new-found respect. You see, as my father was trying to get me from the trailer back into the cabin, I said, I smell smoke.

Peggy-Leigh drank more wine.

My father, who was carrying me and trying to open the screen door at the same time said, Probably someone's fireplace. Try not to worry.

I was ten at the time and had perfected worry.

This seemed to make an impression on Ted because he moved his leg to Peggy-Leigh's and left it there.

Peggy-Leigh couldn't blink.

In bed, she said, thinking the right thing to do would be to continue her story, I almost felt safe as the storm seemed to be leaving. I'd try not to fall for that, storms always left the cabin and then circled back just as I was about to eat something, or to fall asleep, fooled again. I crawled further into my sleeping bag. Tried not to touch any part of the metal bunkbed. Took my earrings out. And worried about fillings.

Ted said, You poor thing, and then he poured Peggy-Leigh more wine.

She couldn't remember having had the first glass.

And then my father came crashing back into the cabin.

Get the operator, Iris, he yelled. The place on the point is on fire.

Ted placed another piece of pizza on her plate. She realized she must have eaten the first. She wondered what the salty bits were.

I was right, Peggy-Leigh said. I gloated to myself for less than a second, and then started to cry again. My mother and father were talking to the operator and then to each other. Then my father came into the bedroom.

Uncle Keith's gone up there. It's okay, he said helping me sit up. You're safe.

I was hiccuping by this point.

Then my father asked, Do you want to go up and look at it with me?

I thought he was nuts. But I couldn't talk.

He said, You'll see, by the time we walk there, the volunteer fire guys will already be working. Come on.

And at that point Peggy-Leigh noticed that her professor had eaten five pieces of pizza. There was one left. She had had two, and couldn't justify more, even when he offered it to her, and even when she knew she would get rid of what she'd eaten soon, so she realized it was maybe time to go. But she didn't know where.

Ted was pulling out his credit card. Peggy-Leigh was impressed. Her parents didn't have any. They didn't believe in them, they said. And she had wondered how she would pay for her share, she hadn't counted on wine and had little money to fool around with, her scholarship covered only the basics like tuition and room and board.

Do you want to go for a drive? asked Ted.

Peggy-Leigh nodded and wondered if she looked too much like a dog that heard the word, Walk? She loved being a passenger. And she didn't have the chance now that she lived in residence and didn't know anyone. The lights of the city from her room at night seemed to laugh at her, taunting.

His sports car smelled like leather. She wasn't sure if it was his jacket or the seats. Both were brown leather, very rich. Ted had opened the door for Peggy-Leigh. She'd pulled her long skirt inside against her legs. Her new black boots her mother wouldn't like, she thought. Derek's football jacket was ripping in one arm, she pulled at it to make it bigger.

Fuck him, she said just as Ted was closing his door.

Excuse me? he said turning to her.

Oh, nothing, Peggy-Leigh said. She was angry with herself for still being angry with Derek and Pam. That was done. Graduation was a black hole she would not go down again.

Go down. The words held her. Derek had said them to her in March of their last term in high school.

I want to go down on you, he said in the guest room of his mother's new condominium. His mother was out with her new boyfriend who was twenty years younger than her.

Peggy-Leigh figured later that at the time she'd been so confused by Derek's parents' break-up and by the new wealth Derek's mother seemed to have, that she'd guzzled the champagne Derek had poured her. She didn't know how many glasses, how many pretty slim-stemmed crystal goblets she'd had. The shape reminded her of Imogene so then she had to have another glassful.

And somehow they'd landed in a small room. The new off-white carpet stank. Peggy-Leigh was lying on it and Derek was on top of her. A small bedside lamp brightly shone. There was no question of lying on the bed, thought Peggy-Leigh, who didn't drink before this and who didn't want to do anything more than neck with her football-playing boyfriend. She loved kissing him. Loved the way he bit her lip gently. Sometimes he sucked it. She could taste peppermint. He was trying to hide the cigarettes, she knew he was thinking of her. His moustache felt like Barbie's hair when, as a kid, Peggy-Leigh had run it against her mouth.

Let me go down on you, Derek said.

Peggy-Leigh remembered the sound of each word by itself. She stared at her boyfriend who was shaking on his elbows as he continued to prop himself up over her. She couldn't have this discussion again.

The worst part was, she didn't know what he was asking.

Down where? she wanted to ask.

Down on me how?

She could hear Elton John lyrics in her head and could smell champagne and carpet glue.

I can't, she said.

Jesus Christ, Derek said.

And then he'd started to cry. He actually started to cry, she thought, as if this was something already in her past she was reflecting on.

They moved apart from one another. Peggy-Leigh did up her top. Derek moved his Levi's, specifically his crotch, away from where it had been touching her body.

And then he'd said he was going to ask Pam, her best friend, to go to graduation.

We can go to my place, Ted was saying. You probably don't get off campus much.

What a gentleman, thought Peggy-Leigh. So mature.

Let's, she said. I can finish telling you about the fire.

As they rode in his car, Peggy-Leigh continued talking. Her mouth felt funny, not in a bad way, she decided. Her tongue seemed happy, if that was the word. She thought it was as if it kept opening her lips with any old words as if just to say, Hi.

She said, He wrapped a blanket around the T-shirt and shorts I'd gone to bed wearing, and remembering I liked to wear them when it stormed, asked if I wanted my gum boots. He knew I wanted to be grounded. We put them on.

Peggy-Leigh studied Ted's hand on the gearshift. Once in a while it would sit on her skirt, on her knee.

So, she continued as they drove along a parkway, outside our cabin, the air smelled like a hundred bonfires. It was dark and surprisingly warm. I hung onto my father harder than I had to. I don't know what I was afraid of. Or I didn't know then, she corrected.

We walked along the dirt road, up the hill, around the corner. I could see flames. Two trucks, other cottagers standing around. I kind of went hysterical.

My father handed me to my mother. Iris, do something with her, he said.

Sweetie, she said. What are you afraid of?

I was hiccuping again and between gulps said, *I think I caused it.* And then wailed away.

Ted's hand was bunching up her skirt. Peggy-Leigh watched the elephants, trees, birds and flowers all squeeze together on the Indian cotton, as if something was approaching their jungle.

My mother laughed. At the time, I was insulted. Angry. Embarrassed. But that lasted seconds. Then, having dealt with those emotions, which distracted from my fear Peggy-Leigh said, hoping it sounded humanities enough.

Humanitarian enough? she wondered.

I was fine. Actually liked the excitement. My mother put me down, I held her hand, we watched the fire and I tried to think of it as just bigger than the one my father built in the rock firepit. There was a kind of beauty to it, which other people recognized because they came from the other side of the lake to watch. Boats motored over and tied at the dock of the cottage that was burning. It was like a big party, Peggy-Leigh said, her voice rising and her left hand grabbing Ted's leather arm almost in spite of herself.

People laughed, yelled, talked. Things were dandy for a while. Imogene had Janis by the hand and they were pretending to be reporters for Bay Lake's *Listener*. That was the name of the paper, she told Ted who took her hand.

Imogene asked all the questions. The cottagers played along. Janis pretended to write with a pretend pencil and pretend paper. My father came by once to see how I was doing. He gave me his one-armed hug and said, We shoulda listened to you, you were right. I felt good. Like a hero of sorts.

Peggy-Leigh looked at the lights they were driving past. She couldn't tell where the lights ended and the stars began.

And then Uncle Keith came running. Where's the mother? he said.

Who? I wondered.

That guy there says a young mother and her newborn were living here, he said.

Peggy-Leigh realized Ted was staring at her and that he had parked the car in front of townhouses with gates and spotlights. We all froze, she said.

Ted kissed her hand.

She wondered why she hadn't wondered before if he was married. Are you married? she asked.

No, he said.

Uncle Keith said, There's no way they woulda got out.

Do you want to go inside? asked Ted gently. I can make us some tea.

She nodded.

Peggy-Leigh was still nodding as Ted opened her door and almost lifted her up and out of the low car. He escorted her along the walkway, which was marked by tiny lanterns.

I didn't want to cry, said Peggy-Leigh once they were inside. Instead, I felt sick, throw up kind.

I spit on the door handle, Ray, my uncle said, when we first got up here, and it sizzled.

I knew this to be a bad sign, said Peggy-Leigh as Ted led her to the couch and sat her down. He took off her leather jacket which said Roughriders. His hand held it where it was ripped.

I pulled my blanket back around where it had slipped off, Peggy-Leigh said.

Ted went to start the kettle.

He couldn't touch the door, Peggy-Leigh said, hoping her voice would carry to wherever the kitchen was. The whole place was too hot. He called and called, no one answered.

Maybe they're not home, I said.

Everyone turned and looked at me.

Peggy-Leigh said, when Ted returned to the living room without his leather jacket or his tie, I was right again.

Ted momentarily stumbled.

But we wouldn't know that till the next day, she said. Meanwhile, I went back to bed, and took Imogene and Janis with me. I heard our parents come in about an hour later. And then I fell asleep.

Ted put two mugs and a teapot on the small glass table.

Peggy-Leigh thought, Wow, glass.

She kept up with her story. She was grateful Ted wanted to listen, she couldn't remember the last time she'd talked this much, certainly not at home. Of the three girls, she talked the least. It was too much trouble, she figured.

I woke suddenly scared. I called for my mom. Nothing.

Dad? I said, wondering briefly if that was the right thing to do having made it clear he was my second choice. No answer.

Shut up, said Imogene.

Ted handed a warm mug to her. He held her hand holding the mug for an instant.

Peggy-Leigh thought she should leave her hand there, but the mug was beginning to burn her skin. She stood it as long as she could.

I got out of bed and looked at her in the top bunk. I couldn't sleep up there, even though everyone knows the oldest gets to, because sometimes I fell out of my bed in Willow Junction.

Where are they? I asked her.

What? she said.

I realized she wasn't really awake. As I said, I move in my sleep, Peggy-Leigh said.

Ted smiled at this.

But Imogene talked. You could have a whole conversation with her while she was asleep, explained Peggy-Leigh. The next morning she wouldn't know a thing. When Mom and Dad would come back from the MTO Christmas party, Imogene would ask all kinds of questions as they kissed her goodnight. She'd want to see the stuff from the table Mom got to take home. One year it was a wax igloo. I'd hear the two of them talking down the hall. Janis shared a room with Imogene and never heard a thing. I would be wide awake not wanting to miss anything. I'd stay awake for a long time after. I'd hear my parents' closet door open, hangers, the door close. I'd hear their bed creak as my father sat to take off his socks. The click of the light as my mother returned from the bathroom. Her wedding and engagement rings landing in their porcelain dish by the bed.

Halfway through this part, Ted had fiddled with the button on her top. It was a cotton, ribbed thing. Long sleeves. Peggy-Leigh remembered she bought it a year earlier because it reminded her of the ballet leotard Imogene wore. She always looked so thin. Benny seemed to notice her. He never notices me, thought Peggy-Leigh.

Ted undid one small black button. There were about ten, in a skinny row, over Peggy-Leigh's breasts, down her stomach.

Okay? he said softly.

She nodded.

Imogene heard nothing, you know? No noise from their room, and none of the conversation she'd had with my parents.

Ted had all the buttons undone.

So she was no help when my parents were missing the night of the fire. Just as I was trying to decide whether to walk up to the burned cottage in my Barbie pyjamas, which I was still wearing three years after I'd got them – the bottoms looked like long shorts and the elastic cuffs of the top were up over my elbows – my parents came back.

Peggy-Leigh had slid her sleeves up to demonstrate.

Ted kissed her wrists.

Apparently the fire had started up again, my mother had seen the glow when she got up to pee, and they'd called the volunteers back and walked up to see if they should do anything.

I was awake the rest of the night, she said.

Still facing her, Ted slid his hand through the opening in her top.

Peggy-Leigh could tell his warm hand was surprised she wasn't wearing a bra. She didn't any more. They didn't fit, they were all too big, the ones she'd worn when she was with Derek.

Ted kissed her.

She felt his tongue and missed Derek's. She hadn't let herself think like that for ages. She had concentrated on other things like calories, laxatives, and when she could get in a washroom when there was no one around who would hear her.

But this tongue is nice, she thought as she moved closer to Ted. I know what I'm doing, I'm a university girl now, she told her new thinner self.

I want to go down on you, whispered Ted.

The fat girl reappeared. Peggy-Leigh stopped moving and looked at the man who had the best voice, she thought, when he lectured. The little microphone clipped onto his stylish blazer, as he talked about famous writers that Mr Elliott, teacher and yearbook faculty adviser, *that* Mr Elliott, had a year earlier talked to her and, she thought, *only* her about. The microphone let him speak softly. Almost in whisper, but all five hundred students seemed to hear or not to care, Peggy-Leigh had noticed as she wondered if her response to him was the same as every other female's.

Do you want that? he asked still cupping her breast.

How could she answer? she wondered suddenly miserable. How could she know what he meant?

She thought of how Imogene seemed more fearless than her. What would Imogene do now? she wondered.

Finally, the thin voice seemed to come out of her and said, I don't know how.

Peggy-Leigh watched Ted look at her. At her eyes. Then her earrings, all of them. He moved his hand from her breast.

I can show you, he said.

And, moments later, Peggy-Leigh had a crazy urge to laugh. She couldn't recall the last time she'd laughed. The last time she threw up? The last time she weighed herself? Sure. But she felt like laughing, really laughing, because, as Ted went about showing her, this insane voice kept asking, Is that all?

And Nothing But The Truth

•

The truth of it was, she'd skipped so many natural science lectures, she wasn't surprised when, at nine o'clock, she opened the heavy lecture theatre door and found the big hall empty. These kinds of things happened to Peggy-Leigh.

Surely, she thought, there's some other idiot like me who will appear here having skipped for a month, and who will know what to do or who to ask. She looked around. At times like this she wished she'd gone on the orientation tours instead of hiding in her room. She'd heard what they did to first-year students.

Be a body part, they'd say.

Or they'd tie a boy and a girl together and make them carry something in their mouths. No, not her, she'd lock her door to the room she shared. Lock it for the whole week if she had to.

If she'd attended even one event maybe she'd know where she should go now, what she should do. She'd know where the department was. What *was* the department? she wondered.

And still no other student showed up. Where was Marcus?

Marcus had asked her out the last time she'd been in class. He had the reddest hair she'd ever seen. He wore brightly coloured button-down shirts, which were always ironed. Peggy-Leigh would stare at the crease on his sleeve for most of the lecture. Some days the crease was a tiny floral. Sometimes it was solid blue. Other times it was the colour and pattern of bricks. She found herself wanting to touch his sleeve. Even more, she had an almost overpowering desire to tear off a piece of the beautiful fabric, run back to her room and stash it.

I'd have enough to make a wall by now, she thought. Maybe that was why she failed the first test. The line of the crease was so perfect. How did his shirts get like that?

She didn't know how to iron. It seemed to be genetic, her mother couldn't or wouldn't iron either. Peggy-Leigh couldn't even manage a curling iron.

Her mother had been right when she said, You'll burn your forehead, I'm not getting you one.

It looked like a hickey, Peggy-Leigh thought as she lifted her bangs and stared into the bathroom mirror. Janis was banging on the bathroom door. In the hallway she shouted, *I have to gooooooooooooo.*

The other bathroom door, the one into their parents' bedroom, was being pounded on by Imogene. *I have ballet!* she yelled, I need my bobby pins!

Peggy-Leigh was sure she could see a pair of lips and teeth marks where her forehead should have been. It was worse than the zits which were usually there. She would have to have bangs her whole life, she decided then. No way she could be like Gillian Morrison who ran her hands through her all-one-length hair at least twenty times a day. Peggy-Leigh would count how many girls watched. Sometimes she counted boys who watched. Sometimes the teacher would watch, especially if it was art class. Mr Moore was not married.

Well, I'll be go to hell, Peggy-Leigh said into the mirror.

She thought that's what her father said once in a while like when he'd just poured his cereal in the morning and then added milk but not enough. Most likely Imogene had just emptied it. There would be no more when her father went to the fridge. It would be a dark day.

She tugged at her bangs. They gapped in places and you could see the purple-red mark like a creature through trees. Peggy-Leigh thought about using Vaseline to stick her bangs to her forehead. If they were straight down and didn't move, maybe no one would know she'd just given herself third-degree burns. She didn't know whether her burn was a third-degree one or not, she just knew the newspaper said things like that.

I'll shellac them, she told her reflection. Like in art last week.

They'd cut pictures out of magazines and had made collages on jars. Once all the faces or flowers had been fixed onto the glass, you were supposed to paint some clear stinky stuff over the whole surface.

Peggy-Leigh's collage hadn't quite turned out the way she

thought it would. She'd carefully cut her pictures out. She was mostly concentrating on colour, she liked red. There was also a lot of blue. Some black, some white. She was always last to finish in art so she thought this time she'd hurry. That way she wouldn't have to talk to Mr Moore for so long.

As she slapped on the clear liquid, she realized she had a jar like no one else's.

It was because, almost too late for the bus, she'd grabbed the first magazine she saw. It was the Sears catalogue.

It should work, she thought. There's lots of colour in it.

Mr Moore was always stressing colour, he'd touch Peggy-Leigh's sleeve and say, What a lovely Hugh.

Mostly she just covered her work with her other arm so that her teacher couldn't see until it was finished. She hated when teachers looked over her shoulder. Sometimes when they did that she'd put her head down and pretend to nap. The teacher would walk on, shaking his head.

The students at her table were staring at her jar.

You're gonna get in trouble, said Claire.

Peggy-Leigh was seeing her creation for the first time. She'd started with boy's wear and must have moved into men's.

Unfortunately, the paper overlapped in less than ideal places. It seemed there were no faces, no limbs, really only one area seemed to be featured.

Peggy-Leigh was fascinated. She'd never looked at it before.

Whatever *it* is, she thought. She looked closer.

Mr Moore cleared his throat behind her left ear. Leaning over, he said, Come with me.

He picked up the offending jar and carried it while Peggy-Leigh followed him into the hallway. The students silently watched the jar of crotches leave.

Anything wrong at home? Mr Moore began.

And she hadn't been able to think of anything that he might be looking for. She surrendered, embarrassed by the collection on the jar.

This will not help my grade, she thought. And she found herself looking down at the floor.

But on the way down, as Mr Moore talked about appropriateness, she lifted her gaze a bit, focused on his fly, and had a good look. Peggy-Leigh looked at her shiny bangs. She imagined they were the Great Wall of China they'd read about in history. Flat and dark, they reflected the little lights around the mirror.

Maybe they look just as good as they would have looked curled, she told herself.

What? screamed Imogene.

In a minute, Peggy-Leigh screamed back.

And she burned her hand on the curling iron.

Go to hell, she told it, and felt good then.

But as she unplugged it she felt guilty for swearing at it, after all, it wasn't really its fault, she thought as she picked it up by the safe handle and sniffed it. It smelled funny, she thought.

But maybe that's the way these are supposed to smell.

The blue handle was pretty. The weight felt good in her right hand. Her prize.

She'd told her mother she was going to win.

I don't want first prize or second. I'm going to win the curling iron, she said. Because you won't buy me one.

They're dangerous, said Iris who'd come to pay and pick up Peggy-Leigh at The Hair Hut.

Peggy-Leigh made a face.

Fine, said Iris, you go ahead and win one.

And sure enough, when they'd come back from Christmas in Toronto, the mail included a notice saying Peggy-Leigh had won third prize and could she come and claim it.

So far, it had been a disaster. She had no one to show her how to use it. Her hair got caught in the barrel and ripped out. Or it seemed to be burning. Once, when she was sure it was in the right way and that things were finally working, she'd removed the wand only to see her bangs bend and shoot skyward. She screamed.

I must have curled them backwards, she said to her angry reflection. And then said, Well, I'll be go to hell.

When Marcus spoke to her the first time, Peggy-Leigh followed the neat crease from cuff to elbow, elbow to shoulder, and then looked at his face. His freckles reminded her of cinnamon and her stomach growled.

That made her mad. She hated when her stomach made loud noises, like it was trying to force her to eat. She thought it was saying, I will embarrass you so much in the classroom or lecture that you will either have to run away or eat before you attend, suit yourself.

Fuck off, she would tell it.

But sometimes she would be afraid not to eat and she would and then she would miss most of what the professor was talking about anyway because she would be doing calorie counts in her head. She'd never liked math before but now it was suddenly useful. She'd multiply and divide and then realize everyone else was packing up their books.

Would you like to go out sometime? he asked.

Peggy-Leigh looked beside and behind her. Me?

He smiled yes. Oh, he said, I'm Marcus. I know your friend Alexis.

Did she have a friend named Alexis?

She lives on your floor, he said. Richmond Hall?

Oh, right, Alexis.

Peggy-Leigh didn't know anyone on her floor. Just the other day someone asked her if she'd just moved in at Thanksgiving but she'd been there since Labour Day.

Yes, she'd said, I *did* just move in.

And then she'd waited for the girl to leave the washroom. And she calmly walked into the part of the bathroom that had a real door, floor to ceiling, that locked.

Inside was a tub and shower. She ran the water as if drawing a bath, and vomited up the bran muffin and orange she'd had for breakfast. The food bits mixed with the water in the tub.

It reminded her of baking, of Imogene's Easy Bake Oven years ago, and the little tins you mixed the mix in with water. The colours, orange and brown were not bad. Lately she'd begun paying attention to what she ate, keeping in mind she'd see it again very soon. Some things had been real mistakes. Anything with red, like ketchup or tomatoes of any kind made her think that she was bleeding.

Maybe she'd torn her throat? Maybe she was bleeding internally? But when she lived after a few of these episodes, she realized she was over-dramatizing. But still, she preferred things like ice cream. It was ideal. Easy to eat, it tasted good, it seemed familiar, it was clean and white going in and coming out. She tried to eat smooth foods from then on when she had to eat. Peanut butter wasn't too bad and her mother kept sending her some.

Are you eating well? she would write. How is the food?

Wet, Peggy-Leigh thought, it's having a bath.

She'd watch it drain away. She'd run water a bit longer, use a disinfecting cleanser and rinse the tub really well. She'd learned that as long as you threw up fairly soon after eating, there was no sick smell. Nothing had fermented. She figured her science course could probably explain it, maybe it already had, and she hadn't been there.

Before she left the little locked room, she would listen to hear if anyone else was in the bathroom's main area. Usually she got up early enough so that no one was around and she could get rid of breakfast fairly easily. No one saw her exiting as if having had a bath fully clothed. After dinner she'd go in in her bathrobe, as if having a leisurely bubble bath which she did in fact have, after having freed dinner, if she'd had dinner.

But one morning, carrying her towel, as she unlocked the door to the tub, she ran into Christa. Peggy-Leigh knew her name because it was on Christa's door, surrounded by sickening hearts.

Excuse me, said Peggy-Leigh, trying to get away quickly.

She brushed passed Christa and ran smack into a hairy man. He was only wearing underwear, blue.

Hi, he said. I'm Stewart.

And he reached past Peggy-Leigh for Christa's hand.

Who's this? he asked his girlfriend. We haven't been properly introduced.

But Peggy-Leigh had fled down the hall to her room before introductions could be made.

That's it, she said, I'm not going to classes today.

Because really, she thought, it's supposed to be an all-girls floor, that's why I requested it, *So why is he here half-naked?*

She thought the bulge in his underwear seemed pretty big.

When her roommate asked why she wasn't going to class, Peggy-Leigh said she had her period. Her roommate looked at her. Maybe she'd said she had it last week too.

Who cares? thought Peggy-Leigh. Well, I'll be go to hell, she chanted.

The freckles moved. He must be saying something, she thought. Pay attention.

Dinner? Marcus said.

What about dinner? asked Peggy-Leigh.

I said I wondered if you'd like to have dinner with me on Friday.

I'd love to, she said and wondered how her stomach had learned to talk.

Great. I'll park in front of your building at six. Look for a blue BMW.

Whatever that is, she thought miserably and smiled.

So Help Me

•

Maybe Marcus dropped the course, he hated me that much.

Peggy-Leigh considered this and looked down the empty corridors. No students were going to come and help her out. This was her own personal hell. Where could they be?

And then a horrible thought hit her in the pit of her empty stomach. Mid-term.

The course outline she'd lost had said something about a big test partway through the term.

Today is about halfway, she calculated. I'm dead.

Long ago, the professor had explained that when there was a mid-term, the students would be divided into several rooms throughout the campus, to avoid the university-wide problem of cheating. There were to be at least two desks between each student. Peggy-Leigh felt sick. It still surprised her that she could feel nauseous, even when she was throwing up already. Somehow, she thought if she was making herself vomit, and was in control of that, her body shouldn't be able, on its own, to make her vomit. Where is the logic? she thought.

She had to do something. Standing outside an empty lecture theatre was just making her feel bad about herself. She thought of Marcus, and that made her feel worse.

He'd arrived in the blue car, which apparently was a BMW. She'd worried all day about the date. Why am I doing this? she kept asking the figure in the mirror in whatever outfit out of twenty it was wearing at that moment. The all-black one. Or the casual jeans and white shirt one – but she couldn't wear that. Think about it, she scolded herself, there are no creases in the arms!

I'm doing this because this is what you are supposed to do in university, stupid, she said.

She liked when her roommate wasn't there. Peggy-Leigh could talk more then. Cynthia had gone to classes for a change. She had a big painting to turn in, and a sketch, and an art history report. She liked to leave things to the last minute and had been working for forty-eight hours straight. The overhead light in their room hadn't been off since sometime Wednesday. At these deadline times, Cynthia worked through the nights while Peggy-Leigh tried to fall asleep. As Cynthia sketched, the pencil made a whispery sound. Peggy-Leigh imagined leaves blowing around on the lawn back in Willow Junction. They swirled in the middle of the grass and then would drift to the edges and rest against the fence. She watched the leaves in her head and couldn't doze. Usually then she would get out of bed and ask if there was any small piece of the work she could do. If she was going to be sleepless, she wanted to be doing something. It was better than thinking, she'd decided. Better than just listening to the seven chocolate-bar wrappers being torn off while Cynthia tried to caffeinate herself awake.

You can push-pin this pile of coloured paper onto the masonite, said Cynthia without looking up from her sketch called *City's-cape*. It should kinda look like this picture when we're done. Leave the pieces the size they are, we can tear them smaller when we get them all on.

Later, Marcus had told Cynthia, whom he apparently knew along with Alexis, whoever she was, that the date hadn't gone well.

For starters, he said, your roommate doesn't eat much. I spend forty bucks on an appetizer and an entree she hardly touched. She may be made of money. And I am too, but waste is waste, he said.

Taking the moral high ground, thought Peggy-Leigh, when she heard.

She'd been a nervous wreck throughout dinner. The restaurant was elegant, perched on a hill overlooking the lights of everything she didn't know. They reminded her of one of Cynthia's collages. As she lifted her water glass and looked through, she thought, There, now I've lacquered it.

A zillion utensils threw her. The waiter placing the linen napkin on her long, formless, floral dress had made her jump and spill her water.

It got worse.

Because she was so nervous about the date and about eating

twice in the same day, her hands shook. Her knife became a spear.

Maybe my unconcious is trying to murder Marcus, she thought.

She tried to divide her food with just her fork. The steak wouldn't cut. If only I could tear it with my hands, she thought, and really missed the simplicity of ripping images from magazines for one of Cynthia's last-minute assignments. The failing grade for glossy magazines apparently not being 'lightfast' meant that on a later night they'd even torn apart some library book matte renderings of Picasso and Matisse. Peggy-Leigh hadn't cared – it wasn't as if *she* was ever going to go into the library.

The rice sat there. Be rice paper, she silently commanded, and I'll glue some steak to you and then brush you with a little vegetable glaze and be done.

She sighed. Goddamn him for insisting I have a steak.

She was worried. She'd never tried to throw up steak. The vision of the dorm bathroom calmed her as she imagined herself back there. She looked at her watch and realized too late that Marcus was watching.

Want to get out of here? he said.

But he'd said it kindly, so she said, Yes, please.

And then they'd gone for a pleasant drive. She thought she recognized some of the streets Ted had driven her down.

Down, there was that word again. Peggy-Leigh opened her electric window. Then she did it up. Then she opened it again. The noise felt like the inside of her head.

We could take the top down, said Marcus.

At first she thought he'd said, We could take your top down.

Peggy-Leigh looked at him.

Or we could drive north a bit, to a look out I know. It's a bit cooler up there.

Look out! she thought.

She stopped the wind from running through her brush cut. It didn't move even in the strongest breeze. She liked that, it always looked the same, she never looked like she had screwed-up her hair with a hair dryer or curling iron. The girls in her hallway were always walking around with curlers in their hair in the middle of the afternoon. They watched soaps and got ready for their evening dates. All their classes were in the afternoon so that they could sleep in after drinking and doing whatever else they did at night.

Why are you here? Peggy-Leigh wanted to ask several of them as she overheard them in the common room talking about finding parking spots for their 280 z xes, or complained about their mothers who phoned and yelled at them about seven-hundred-dollar charge statements from Holt Renfrew.

Holt, again, she would think. What was seven hundred dollars?

A sweater and slacks for Friday night, apparently. And lunch at the restaurant there for Sidra, Molly, Eve and Gaby.

So, much later, it seemed to Peggy-Leigh that all the girls on her floor knew Marcus, except her. Or knew *about* him, was perhaps more accurate, she decided. They'd driven for about thirty minutes while listening to a tape.

The Alan Parsons Project, said Marcus.

A project for school? wondered Peggy-Leigh.

She nodded and suddenly nervously wondered if she was Marcus's project. She couldn't help thinking about grade twelve biology and Mr Curtis and the heart she couldn't dissect.

The formaldehyde actually made her hungry. She knew she was in trouble then. As she carried the beige-coloured organ on a paper towel back to her station, she thought of food. The little tray she placed it on didn't help. It looked just like one her grandmother used to bake Shake-and-Bake chicken on. Peggy-Leigh's stomach let out a moan. Tears came.

And there was Curtis the Flirtis taking her elbow before she even could put down her project.

Let's talk in my back room, he said.

She felt faint. She also felt afraid she'd slice the heart with her little dissecting knife and then would stick the piece in her mouth.

You don't have to do this, you know, Mr Curtis said, amid test tubes and beakers in the secret room.

There was paper everywhere. Peggy-Leigh saw the grade book and quickly scanned for her name. Her watery grades rippled. Eighty-five. And then, forty.

Do what? asked Peggy-Leigh.

Mr Curtis was holding her hand. He looked at her without saying anything.

Do what? she asked again thinking maybe she'd only asked it in her head the first time.

He sighed. What's going on? he asked. You can tell me.

Nothing, I guess I'm allergic to the preservative stuff.

She wiped her eyes so that she could take her hand back.

Something's going on, he said. You don't go from honours down to failing without a reason.

The leaf project was easier, she said. And that stuff about plant cells and animal cells I just memorized.

Do I have to call your parents in?

What for? she asked very worried. I can dissect this thing, piece of cake, she said.

This scared her too.

Don't bother today, he said.

He took both of her hands. His were warm and she realized hers were freezing.

Take this period off, he said. You'll have to make this up later.

Alan Parsons had ended sometime and 'Stairway to Heaven', one of the longest songs in history, was on the car stereo.

Bad camp memories came wafting in the closed windows.

Ten fucking minutes, she thought.

And she always ended up dancing with someone who didn't speak English and who wanted to tongue her as if this would make up for not being able to talk.

I might be in trouble, she thought. What will Marcus want to do? He had wanted to do various things. As she stared through the front windshield at the village below, she almost didn't care. The view was incredible. The air was fresh, Marcus had rolled all the windows down, and she could hear the trees. How she'd missed that sound, she hadn't realized until now.

Come here, he said. I'll keep you warm.

Then he said, Bring your garden closer.

Peggy-Leigh hoped he was referring to the print on her dress. As she moved over to him, a lot of the flowers stayed near the door on her side. The dress was that big.

Marcus reached under his seat and brought out a wrinkled copy of *Playboy*.

Now what? wondered Peggy-Leigh thinking she'd truly been very stupid. Think fast.

Marcus was fiddling with his belt.

I have to tell you something, she said.

Marcus smiled. It won't hurt you, I promise, he said.

I have VD, she said.

His look changed immediately.

VD was all she could think of. She wasn't sure what it was, she'd seen a film in grade twelve health class which had helped her not want to eat lunch that day. There were a lot of things she couldn't remember when she tried to recall them lately. She hoped Marcus wouldn't ask her about VD because she kept drawing blanks. She just knew it was bad.

Fuck! he said.

Yes, she said, I thought you'd want to know. He'd driven her back without talking. He was speeding all the way. His marvellously creased striped arm matched the line of his mouth.

At her residence he said, Night.

He flipped up her lock by hitting the panel on his side. And shook his head.

Peggy-Leigh didn't care, she was close to smiling. The bathroom would be empty this time of night.

The week after the missed mid-term, Peggy-Leigh forced herself to go see how bad things were. Sure enough, all five hundred students showed up for Plants Are People Too. It was officially called Plants and People, but was known by its other name and was known to be the easiest of all the required sciences.

She was shaking as she sat near the back. But she often shook, this was nothing too bad. Sometimes she was cold. Sometimes she just shook. She knew enough not to drink tea after not having eaten for a day or so, she really shook then. And shaking wasn't as bad as feeling dizzy and losing her hearing.

Last time that happened she was in the gigantic library, in all its unfinished concrete glory, hunting material for Cynthia.

It literally stinks, she thought to herself as she stared at the open-concept hell.

She saw the escalator and lots of students going up it so she thought that's what she should do.

It was a long ride up.

This must be what a mine shaft is like, she thought.

She thought of her relatives who'd worked the mine in New Liskeard. How did they do it?

Panels of lights on either side lit up and flashed off and lit up again.

Must be malfunctioning, she thought. I hope I get off soon.

Words slid past her. *Installation*, they kept saying. *Touch me*, others kept saying.

She was getting dizzy. *Touch, touch, touch,* kept chanting in her head. Peggy-Leigh put her right hand out to steady herself. She hit a metal strip, which must have sensed something. Lights flashed wildly and the escalator seemed to speed up and the people going down seemed all to be mouthing the word *down*. She could see the landing, the end of the powered stairs, but at the same time seemed to be falling.

Right at the top, she passed out.

What seemed like a short time later, she opened her eyes and saw carpet. She was lying on her stomach on the carpet. She could hear the escalator hum. People were stepping over her.

Maybe they think I'm a drama major, she thought.

She stayed there a moment longer, having rolled over, to look at footwear trends and brand names while trying to decide if crawling over to the wall was possible. It was. She did after counting seven different tread patterns. The lines were interesting. She sat there, leaning against the cold concrete, looking at the bottom of her own shoes and vowing to eat something before she next came into the library.

Better yet, she thought, I just won't come back at all.

In her seat, the shaking seemed to subside a bit. I'm just nervous about missing the test, she told herself. It's not physical.

Her professor looked nervous too. She paced right and left at the front of the big room. The large woman rubbed her fat hands together. Peggy-Leigh thought of diets.

I have something to say, the professor said.

Well, we *are* scheduled to be here two hours, thought Peggy-Leigh. Of course you have something to say.

This has never happened in my twenty-five years of teaching.

No one's ever missed the mid-term, thought Peggy-Leigh horrified. I'm about to be stoned at the front of the room.

I've lost your exams, said Dr Rogers.

There was gasping, swearing, and a lot of talking.

Peggy-Leigh was thanking God.

The girl beside her said, And it was so fucking simple!

Yes, said Peggy-Leigh.

So I'm afraid I can't count it, said Dr Rogers. We'll write one again in two weeks.

God

•

As she walked from the Wellesley subway station, Peggy-Leigh told herself, Be a trained seal.

She hoped that at the party she would be able to laugh in the right places, after the punch-line and not before, and not too late after. Drinking, too. Knowing when to drink and how much always baffled her. It didn't help that when faced with social drinking, she'd usually had nothing to eat that day. Or at least, nothing that remained in her body long enough to turn into energy or calories or whatever it was supposed to turn into. One beer was usually more than enough, but no one believed her. Sometimes she had to pour them into plants when no one was looking, these gifts of beer people would hand her. Here, have another, they'd say. She heard it as an order, always. How many plants had she killed? She felt worst about cactuses.

Her grandmother had given her three plants from hers for her eighth birthday. They liked to be dry. You hardly ever watered them. That's why she was allowed to have them – her mother didn't think she'd kill them like she'd kill real plants. Probably right, Peggy-Leigh thought back then, having just recently put a rug over Imogene's head, which had led to disastrous results.

Peggy-Leigh had tried to invent a new game. The object was to find the fireplace in the rec room. The searcher wore a rug over her head. The other person pointed the blinded one in the right direction and watched. A table and footstool had been removed so that the seeker would not trip.

And the game was working fine. Imogene walked with her arms straight out, like Frankenstein, thought Peggy-Leigh, towards the dark bricks.

And then their mother had called. Peggy-Leigh, come up here.
Now?
Right now.

Peggy-Leigh didn't think it sounded good. Better go now, before it gets worse, whatever it is, she thought.

She walked up the stairs two at a time, her knees folding and unfolding like the legs on the bridge table her mother had bought a week ago, in case she, Iris, ever learned how to play.

Besides, she'd told everyone when the box arrived from Sears, it was on sale.

Why is my perfume down so low? Iris asked.

She was holding the amber liquid above her head.

I don't know, Peggy-Leigh lied.

I think you do, said Iris.

Why?

Because Janis saw you go into Mommy and Daddy's room yesterday.

I wanted to look out the window in there.

Then she added, I wanted to see if you could see Albert's tree house from there.

That sounded good, she thought.

Janis said it was stinky when you came back out.

Where had Janis been? Peggy-Leigh wondered. In the clothes hamper?

But then there came a terrible shriek from the basement. It sounded as if Imogene was on fire. Peggy-Leigh always thought of fire first, then she examined the other possibilities.

She and her mother ran down the stairs, not holding the railing like they were always supposed to. Either one of them could have fallen, Peggy-Leigh thought, but not for long, the screams were that bad.

The scene had been truly terrifying when they arrived. There seemed to be a lot of blood. It was coming through the rug which was still over Imogene's head. The rug had been turquoise.

It reminds me of the lake, Iris had said when she brought it home the winter before.

The red and turquoise mixed together and made a kind of purple. Peggy-Leigh thought she should remember this for art class.

Her mother had gone to her sister and was trying to hold her still. They were in front of the fireplace. Peggy-Leigh stayed back and tried to figure out how her sister had hit her head. The fireplace shelf at about knee level should have prevented Imogene from hitting her head on the bricks. The cement shelf seemed to come out about a foot.

It should have stopped her, thought Peggy-Leigh.

And then she thought, Well, really, I should have stopped her.

And she'd intended to, really, but then the perfume issue had come up. It wasn't really her fault, she thought, was it? Her mother was trying to get the rug off Imogene's head. Imogene didn't seem to want it off.

It's okay, sweetie, let me have a look.

Peggy-Leigh couldn't look. What if part of her face came off with the rug? She sat down, her legs felt wobbly, like she was on ice with skates that her father hadn't tied tight enough. She imagined her foot between her father's knees as he kneeled in front of her and tugged tight.

Tell me if they're too loose, he'd always say. You can't skate properly if they aren't tight. This is how hockey players tie theirs, he'd say and his finger would trace the part of the lace which he'd threaded through the rest of the criss-cross work.

See? he'd say.

She didn't understand it, but it worked. She'd see other girls who didn't have a lace going diagonally and they would be falling all over the ice, or skating on the sides of their ankles and she'd think, My father is better than your father.

The rug came off. It curled at the bottom of Imogene's feet. The red lines on it looked like snakes.

What did you do? Iris demanded in Peggy-Leigh's direction.

I went upstairs, said Peggy-Leigh, trying not to cry but it didn't work.

Through her beginning tears she said, You called me.

As if it was her mother's fault.

Before that, said Iris, not buying it. What were you doing putting a rug over your sister's head.

Imogene must have told all while Peggy-Leigh had been thinking about skating in Civic Gardens.

Shit, said Peggy-Leigh.

Imogene stopped crying and Iris looked at her oldest daughter. What did you say?

Peggy-Leigh stopped breathing as she realized things were just going from bad to worse.

Sheesh, it. I said. Sheesh, it was supposed to be a game.

Janis had waddled in and was looking at her too.

Find the fireplace, you know?

I'll deal with you later, said Iris. Go find your father outside and tell him what you've done and that I'm taking your sister for stitches. Take Janis with you.

A couple of hours later Imogene had come back perfectly fine. And she had a stuffed bear from the hospital gift shop. Peggy-Leigh watched both her parents fussing over her sister. While she was genuinely glad her sister hadn't bled to death, and that her brains hadn't fallen out, she did wonder about all the attention Imogene was getting. Really, it had just been a game that didn't quite work out, what was all the fuss?

You're grounded, her mother said.

Two weeks, her father added.

Why? thought Peggy-Leigh. It wasn't my fault that Imogene tripped.

The story had come out when they returned from the hospital. Imogene had tripped, possibly on a shoelace she'd tried to tie herself – she was just learning and could get the bunny ears part, her father had showed her often enough, but she didn't know what to do with the bunny ears – she made them and then squashed them together hoping they'd form a knot and bow on their own.

Iris had noticed blood dripping towards the ground when Imogene leaned towards her. The blood made a splotch on an undone shoelace.

So that's how she cracked her head open. It wasn't my fault, thought Peggy-Leigh. It was my mother's for not buying her slip-on sneakers again. She's too little for laces, even I know that! And Peggy-Leigh started to feel better. The whole thing would be forgotten by the time her grounding was over, she was sure. And she could just read in her room until then. Or play Barbie. And maybe come up with a better game than fireplace.

She looked at the fireplace. You couldn't tell where Imogene's head had hit. On the other hand, you could tell where the fireplace had hit Imogene's head. Peggy-Leigh gazed at the spot. There were two really. One had stitches, the ends of which barely stuck out of the skin on Imogene's forehead. The other spot, close to it, had a kind of fancy bandage on it.

Butterfly tape, said Imogene, smiling.

That spot hadn't been deep enough to require stitches, the doctor had said. A butterfly tape would do.

And then Peggy-Leigh was miserable. Imogene got their parents' attention, a new stuffed bear, *and* a butterfly tape.

I get grounded. Everyone's mad at me.

She looked at the silvery tape on her sister's forehead. It didn't look like the orange butterfly she'd caught the summer before. The one that was dead when she opened the jar the next day. Peggy-Leigh felt bad about that. But maybe it was just old?

That's why you died, she told herself as she poured the butterfly into her hand.

It was beautiful. And soft. And she didn't think she should just throw it away.

And besides, she thought in a flash, it's just like the one Pam's dad has in a wooden box in the room with all his adding machines.

She'd tried to make it like the one in the wooden box with the glass cover. She took bulletin-board pins off the cork board near the fridge. She grabbed the small mirror from her bedroom. The back of it was cork, she thought. She took all these materials and the butterfly into the shed. She would try pinning the butterfly to the board. She'd worry about putting glass over it later.

But the operation didn't work. The wings kept shredding. One came right off. And the pins would slip and stick into her fingers. Finally she'd tossed all of it into a garbage can in the shed.

Sorry, she said as she left.

The silvery tape didn't look the least bit like that butterfly. And that, she decided, was probably good.

I didn't mean to, she said to Imogene.

To what?

Hurt your head.

Imogene shrugged her shoulders and had a sip of the root beer float her father had made her. I know, she said. Want to play *bear*? What was she doing going to a party anyway, she asked herself as she pulled her coat closer. Either it is getting more like winter earlier these days, she thought, or I just get cold a lot. Was it always this cold in November?

She tried to remember what the weather was like in Willow Junction. But she didn't try very hard. She didn't really want to remember anything about home lately, it just made her sad and angry and she didn't know why. She spent no time trying to figure out why, it was all she could do to get to some classes, look at the reading assignments, and start and finish her essays the night before they were due.

At a party I'll have to eat. Someone will make me.

These thoughts rose up in front of her as visibly as the white air her breath made.

Then she told herself, Relax. Think of things you can eat which are low-calorie. Be prepared ahead of time and you'll be calmer. Think carrot sticks, celery. You can have mineral water from those lovely green French bottles. One or two crackers with nothing on them. Eat these slowly, so people will think you are eating like everyone else. No potato chips. No cheeses. Stay away from cake.

She repeated these plans silently to herself in time to her walk. People rushed past her and she wondered where were they going on a Saturday night? Maybe the hockey game, it was close, the Leafs were in town. Her father would watch it on TV. This made her sad.

Everything makes you sad, stupid, she told herself while trying to stay warm.

She couldn't figure out if she was hugging herself because of the cold or the sadness. It didn't matter because nothing worked.

Maybe I will eat a little bit, she said. Maybe I'll have to get home. She hated when she realized she had to eat in order to get all the way back to the university from downtown. It was like she'd failed. If anyone had asked her, she would have had to admit, it also scared her that she could be in such a desperate state that she wasn't sure she would be okay.

Okay, she said out loud.

She said it often these days. Like, Okay, let's get going. Or, Okay, I'm okay. Or, Be okay, please be okay. She talked more to herself than she had to anyone in years, she thought.

A party. Why did I say yes?

She could see Pam's apartment building in the distance. She'd been there once since they'd all ended up in Toronto. Pam already had a new boyfriend by then, Pierre. Derek and she had gone to Grad together, and then had seemed to be trying to make it work so that both of them would not see grad as having been a big mistake. At least, that's how Peggy-Leigh saw things. All summer people would tell her they'd seen Derek and Pam at mini-putt, or at the lake, and that they didn't seem happy.

Oh? she'd say. And then she'd decide not to eat lunch. And maybe dinner.

Pam had met Pierre during frosh week, she said when she called Peggy-Leigh in late September. I want you to meet him, she said. A truce, perhaps, thought Peggy-Leigh. She wants it.

So she'd gone there for dinner in October. Lasagna. It had tasted really good and that made Peggy-Leigh want to forgive her friend even less.

Derek lives near here, Pam said.

Do you know Derek? Peggy-Leigh asked Pierre, who was opening another bottle of wine.

No, said Pam. He doesn't.

End of discussion, thought Peggy-Leigh. She doesn't want me to end his delusion that she is a virgin, I guess.

She sipped her wine. How many calories in wine? She made a note to find out the next day.

And so the dinner had gone. Peggy-Leigh liked Pierre. She especially liked him for being not as handsome as Derek. His blond hair hung flat on his head. His eyebrows were a dark bar across his forehead. They reminded Peggy-Leigh of Imogene's hairband when it fell forward.

Maybe Pam likes him for his accent, thought Peggy-Leigh, it's so foreign.

Even if it was only from Québec, Peggy-Leigh knew Pam well enough to know that her friend had convinced herself it was a Paris accent.

Derek will be here, said Pam, when she called with the invitation to her November party.

So? said Peggy-Leigh.

Don't you want to see him?

I heard he's got a girlfriend at Ryerson and she's really beautiful.

Peggy-Leigh didn't actually know anything about Derek's new girlfriend, she just knew there was one. She added the beautiful part to make Pam feel bad.

They'll be here, I think you should come, said Pam.

What the hell for? Peggy-Leigh wanted to shout. Instead she'd agreed. She thought it was her stomach again.

The building looked different somehow to Peggy-Leigh and she hoped she hadn't screwed up again. Twice she'd gotten disoriented on the campus and had been unable to find her class. She'd somehow ended up in the Fine Arts building, surrounded by canvases in the huge main lobby, and she'd been trapped as if in a maze. Not a scary one, or a claustrophobia-inducing one, a serene one, she thought. And there were no students around. On an office door there was a sign, GONE FOR LUNCH, and Peggy-Leigh remembered Cynthia complaining that there was absolutely nowhere to buy food in the Fine Arts building. This is great, Peggy-Leigh said aloud. And then later, having stayed too long, she had trouble finding the strength to walk back to her room in residence. Sometimes her vision blurred.

Maybe I just wasn't paying attention last time.

She didn't remember the strong smell of pee in the stairwell or the cracked pane of glass in the entranceway.

But there was the little card on the door with Pam's name next to Pierre's. Peggy-Leigh wondered about going in but she was cold.

In it is, she said.

Diana wasn't that beautiful. Her long black hair just makes her seem so, thought Peggy-Leigh unhappily. Anyone looks good in long hair, she continued, and thought of Imogene. Maybe I weigh less than her now, she told herself. It's okay.

Diana had turned as Peggy-Leigh walked in. Even though they were a room's distance apart, they both knew who was who without introductions. One look and Diana had turned her back.

I'm not that bad, said Peggy-Leigh under her breath. I could grow my hair back if I wanted to.

But she felt ugly. Really ugly. She could feel a bad ugly attack coming on.

Pam offered her a glass of wine.

Peggy-Leigh's chant about mineral water stayed out in the hallway as she closed the door. There was no escaping now. She'd have that glass of wine, and maybe more, it was going to be a long night, she realized.

Derek appeared and kissed her on the cheek. He didn't like the hair, or the lack of it on her head, she could tell. He stared at her.

Oh, Cub, he said because he'd called her Cub Reporter when she worked on the yearbook. He sounded sad.

She wanted to say, Don't call me that, but she couldn't.

You must be studying too much, he said.

She knew what he was thinking. I'm fine, she said. Sometimes I'm just so busy, you know, with my friends, that I don't have time to eat, that's all.

He shook his head. I missed you, he said.

Well, here I am, she said waving her wine glass in what she hoped was a look of festiveness not hysteria.

You know about Diana? he asked quietly.

Peggy-Leigh didn't think she really wanted to know anything about Diana the Goddess. She tried to look blank at her ex-boyfriend's question. That you're going out?

Derek looked uncomfortable.

Were they or weren't they? Peggy-Leigh wanted to know.

Actually, we're living together.

Peggy-Leigh tried to swallow her wine but wondered if it was still in the glass and was she trying to down one of Pam's chipped glasses.

There was a big screw-up with residence, he said. I met Diana at student housing the day I was supposed to move in. She was out of a room also, so we decided the best thing to do would be to get an apartment.

Of course, said Peggy-Leigh, trying not to writhe.

Paul lives with us, Derek added quickly.

Paul had been Derek's best friend in high school.

As if that makes everything okay, thought Peggy-Leigh.

It's a nice three-bedroom, Derek said.

Who cares, she wanted to say but said, Could you get me another glass of wine?

You drink now? he said and smiled.

She said, Sometimes.

And after he'd gone she said, When it can't be avoided.

The night went slowly. She thought of the hockey game. It seemed to her the action was slow, the game at the party was just shooting from one end to the other with no real good shots on goal. And too many penalties were being called. Just let them play, she said.

Who? said Derek, back again for at least the sixth time.

Peggy-Leigh wasn't sure if she'd meant for Diana and Derek to play, or the rest of the people at the party. She was drunk.

Where's Diana? she asked.

She had to go. She's catching a late bus to Montreal to her parents'.

Oh, too bad, said Peggy-Leigh. I never got to talk to her.

She gulped the last of the wine in her glass. It was white. She thought she'd been drinking red earlier.

Oh well, she said.

Her parents are splitting up, said Derek. It's pretty hard on her.

Yeah, break-ups are hard, said Peggy-Leigh looking toward the kitchen.

What's going on? asked Derek touching her arm.

Peggy-Leigh looked down at his hand. Wasn't that Diana's hand now? What was he doing giving it to her?

You've lost weight, he said.

Those words did funny things to Peggy-Leigh. They made her happy, afraid, angry, and proud, not necessarily in that order. It depended on the day.

GOD

She wanted not to be so fat. She wanted people like her parents to leave her alone about her weight. When they said You've lost weight, it was like, You've been bad, we'll have to do something about that. When the girls on her floor said it, she was proud she could do something they couldn't. Sometimes she was almost sure she was the skinniest on her floor, but then she'd see Sidra having only salad for dinner and she'd get confused. Maybe Sidra was smaller. Maybe, Peggy-Leigh thought, I'm really even fatter than I think and everyone is just being polite.

It's not a problem, said Peggy-Leigh.

Let's go for a walk, said Derek, I'll get your coat.

She'd told him it was blue. She'd had to borrow her roommate's coat because she couldn't wear the football jacket if Derek was going to be there.

Then they were outside in the falling snow.

Let me know if you get too cold, said Derek. We can duck in somewhere for a coffee or hot chocolate.

Coffee, said Peggy-Leigh just to establish that early. Fewer calories, she was thinking.

And so they'd walked. There were small, dead-end streets with dollhouses on them which Peggy-Leigh would never have found on her own. Derek said he lived near.

I knew you'd like it here, he said. He put his arm around her as they slowly walked.

It felt different, his arm around her, but Peggy-Leigh wasn't sure why. Maybe it was the blue coat. Maybe it was the different body, she thought. I traded it in.

The lights in the small houses looked inviting. I want to be inside, she said to herself. I want to be the person who lives here, this one with the shutters.

I always thought we'd get married, said Derek.

Peggy-Leigh inhaled and held her breath.

And we'd live in a house downtown like this.

She exhaled. And have two cars, two point two kids, and a cat and a dog? she asked.

He looked at her. Maybe, he laughed. Didn't you think like that?

Her head was rushing like a waterfall. Must be the booze, she thought. I'm cold, she said.

Here, he said.

And he turned to face her. Then he embraced her, pressing the length of his body against hers. Let me warm you, he whispered to the seven earrings.

She started to cry. She thought it was the cold, the wine, not enough food and too much at the same time, and Diana.

What it is? he said releasing her.

She said nothing.

You're shivering. Let's go. You need a warm drink, I know a place close to here.

He took her hand. He held it for a second then tucked her hand still inside his into his jacket pocket.

Her other hand wanted to be inside too. Don't eat anything there, Peggy-Leigh cautioned herself.

The red and yellow sign welcomed them. Inside it was warm and sweet smelling.

Croissants, said Derek. Have you tried one?

Of course I haven't, she thought. But she just said, No.

Let me buy you one, he said. Please?

Same old song, thought Peggy-Leigh. She was remembering the times in high school when Derek had wanted her to eat. He was worried, always worried it seemed, the last year they were together. You can't make me eat, she would say, fighting.

But she knew he could. Not by what he said. But by how much she loved him and didn't want to hurt him. She could tell she was hurting him, his look said it all and she didn't want to hear. She also knew if he hadn't said he was going to ask Pam to graduation, they would have broken up anyway. Peggy-Leigh was getting more serious about not eating and Derek seemed to be the only thing standing in her way. She'd made him promise early on not to tell anyone that she didn't eat much. And that time she passed out at his grandparents' cottage he was never to mention.

She seemed to have spent a lot of her life making deals with boys, she thought as Derek went up to the counter to order coffees and a chocolate croissant for them to share.

Albert had been the worst. Peggy-Leigh was glad his family had moved. Probably he was in jail by now, having outgrown the reformatory he'd been sent to for stabbing another boy.

It didn't surprise her, Albert's anger. You could always see bones and rage just beneath the surface of his skin, like there wasn't enough skin to hold everything in. Her mother hadn't wanted her to play with him, but her friend Lanny had just moved from the very same house and Peggy-Leigh had cried all week.

Albert and Peggy-Leigh played with matches the first afternoon they played together. They broke a neighbour's clothesline shortly after. The kissing followed at some point.

It had been Albert's idea. You want to practise, he said, so that when a guy you like kisses you you'll know how to kiss back and won't make him sick.

I don't like any guy, she said.

But you will, he said. I don't like you either, you know, I mean like like, but we should know how.

Peggy-Leigh thought his argument made some sense but she still didn't want to kiss Albert.

You know that mini-lighter my brother got in the gum machine? Peggy-Leigh nodded.

I'll give it to you if you kiss me.

It's your brother's, she said avoiding the issue.

He gave it to me.

She had liked the little lighter. It was metal. Red. Small. She liked small things. Albert had said it would really light, it just needed some lighter fluid and he could steal that from his parents. She didn't know about that, if it would light. That wasn't why she liked it and why she was considering kissing Albert. She liked the idea of it. How it felt cool in her hand. And usually you just got junk out of those gum machines.

So she kissed him.

That wasn't long enough, he said. I'm not giving it to you for that.

But someone will see us, Peggy-Leigh said.

That wasn't it. She was afraid she might get in trouble, but mostly she didn't like the feel of his wet lips and he was breathing so hard out of his nose she could feel it on the space between her nose and mouth. The truth was she didn't like it. She didn't like kissing Albert.

Do you want the lighter or not?

It should have been hers already, she thought, and she didn't want to have kissed him that first time for nothing. So she kissed him again and held her face there until he pulled back.

That was better, he said. I'll go get the lighter. Peggy-Leigh was making a list in her head of things she'd earned by kissing Albert, the neighbourhood terrorist. A toy car, a baseball, GI Joe, her own family's Christmas lights which Albert had stolen, a cap gun. She'd never told her father how she got the lights back. Everyone thought Albert had taken them, so she just said, I talked to him.

Try this, Derek was saying. He'd torn off a small piece and was offering it on a napkin to Peggy-Leigh.

A piece of peace, she thought.

The chocolate was leaking, it made Peggy-Leigh think of a wound. But she ate it, and it was good. She thought Derek seemed like quite the city dweller now, knowing about croissants and the dollhouse streets. And he's probably having sex every night.

How's the head now? he asked her.

You mean all the wine I had?

He nodded.

It hurts, she said meaning everything.

Let me walk you back to Pam's, he said. I guess you'd planned to spend the night there?

No, she said thinking that would be pretty awful. I'm going back to campus.

Not at this hour, he said. The trains have stopped.

Really?

She hadn't known, she never would have stayed this late if she had, she was mad at herself now.

Hey, hey, he said looking closely at her. You can stay at my place if you'd rather.

She looked at him as if through a kaleidoscope. He was all colours. Chips of him fell this way and that. She needed her roommate's glue and a big board to stick him to.

Really, he said. Stay.

When she thought about it later, back in her miserable dorm room, there was nothing she could have done differently. So why do I feel so bad?

Maybe I'm going bad, she thought. Any food that I eat and don't get rid of makes me go bad inside.

She believed this.

Derek's apartment was not an apartment, it was part of a house. It seemed like it was half a house. If you cut a house in half, thought Peggy-Leigh, the way you cut a cake, you would get the space Derek and Diana and Paul lived in.

Paul is back home, said Derek as he took the blue coat and hung it up. Back home meant Bay Lake.

He was sorry to miss the party. He said to say hi to you.

Hi back, said Peggy-Leigh looking around and wishing she could hide in the blue coat. Her white sweater, loose, didn't feel elegant any more like she'd hoped, it felt too big.

Damn Diana for wearing form-fitting clothes, she thought.

Peggy-Leigh's skirt could have covered the couch in Derek's living room, it was that big. She'd tied a bandanna as a belt around her waist. This was to remind her not to eat, no matter how hungry she got. It was also the only thing holding up her print skirt.

If this goes, she'd thought as she tied the bandanna in front of the full-length mirror back in her dorm room, so do the vines. She'd meant the ones on her skirt. I'll be stepping out of them around my ankles. I'd better wear a good slip just in case. She hadn't thought the skirt was that big. Must have stretched when I hand-washed it. Maybe I was wringing it, and it's one of the ones you're not supposed to wring.

She arranged the vines around her as she sat on the couch. She thought she should say something about Diana, but what?

Diana seems nice, she said.

I'm an idiot, she told herself.

You'd like her, said Derek.

And you're an idiot too, she silently told him and then asked, Is she studying at Ryerson too?

Fashion, said Derek nodding as he sat across from her on the floor.

He looked smaller than she remembered. His jacket must have hidden this.

We even shared a booth at an exhibition at the beginning of school. Everyone was supposed to show the portfolio that got them in.

What do you show? said Peggy-Leigh.

She'd meant to say, What do you know? but the alcohol had done something.

You, he said.

What?

I show you. You're what got me into Ryerson's photography program.

Peggy-Leigh started shaking a little.

You're cold, he said.

She was trying to decide if this was a statement about her emotional output, or her body temperature. At any rate, he went to get her a quilt, he said.

You don't miss a thing, do you? she thought as she watched Derek's back disappearing down the hallway. She found herself looking forward to the panels of patterned fabric. Perhaps she could steal pieces from the quilt. Maybe Cynthia could use them, she thought. And then, What the hell's wrong with me?

The apartment seemed tall and thin.

Like I want to be, she thought. Trust him to find a place like that.

But Diana didn't seem that thin. Just gorgeous, everything slightly overdone. Hair to her waist. Big breasts. She was probably what guys thought was sexy, Peggy-Leigh decided. Of course she's in fashion.

Derek came back carrying a dark quilt and a funny-looking suitcase that looked like a streetcar had driven over it.

What's that? she asked.

My portfolio. You have to carry them in these, he said.

And then he ran the zipper all the way around. It reminded

Peggy-Leigh of a model train she'd seen long ago in Hugh's basement. Hugh lived on their street. His mother worked and so after school they could eat whatever they wanted. Sometimes they ate brown sugar. With nothing else, just brown sugar in their hands. Then they'd watch the train downstairs or play pool. They didn't use the wooden sticks, they just shot the balls with their hands, Peggy-Leigh and Hugh felt very grown up.

And then one day, Hugh had wiped sugar off on his dirty jeans and had said, Do you want to see it?

What? Peggy-Leigh said licking sugar out of her hand. She felt like a pony eating hay from someone's hand. She liked horses.

My thing.

What thing?

Hugh rolled his eyes. He seemed older than ten then. Peggy-Leigh had seen her father roll his eyes, usually about money.

You know, Hugh said and he pointed to the front of his pants.

Peggy-Leigh stopped licking. Oh, that, was all she said.

She'd never seen one 'and didn't know if she wanted to. GI JOE didn't have anything down there. She had checked.

Here, Hugh said. Let's go into the furnace room.

She didn't like the sound of that but she went. She didn't want Hugh to tell everyone at school that she was chicken.

She watched him undo his pants. He pulled them down to his knees.

Peggy-Leigh didn't know where to look. The concrete floor was cold on her feet. The basement smelled like a basement. When would his mother get home?

Don't you want to look?

Do you want me to?

Peggy-Leigh looked up then and saw that Hugh was wearing blue underwear. She decided then that if she ever got married she'd say to her husband, Wear white.

Hugh was pulling them down too.

She looked. It was small. For some reason she'd been under the impression that it was bigger.

He was holding it out to her. Want to touch?

No, she said, that's okay. Thanks.

She decided she liked watching the train more. The little trees and hydro poles were perfect. She also liked the way the train disappeared into the tunnel and then reappeared while blowing its whistle.

Peggy-Leigh wrapped the blanket around her body. She liked being covered up. Her face wasn't that bad. Sometimes she wished she could just be a face.

Just another pretty face, she said.

What? asked Derek as he looked up from his big portfolio case.

Nothing, she said. I can't believe you got in with pictures of me. I thought you were just goofing around when you took them.

He smiled. I liked to photograph you. I think it shows in the shots, here.

He handed an eight-by-ten to her. It was black and white. She remembered she'd been folding laundry the afternoon he took it. She was wearing a pair of Janis's navy knee socks as long gloves. Her face was framed by her hands, she was leaning on her elbows.

I called this *Laundry at Tiffany's*, he said.

She remembered the movie they'd seen on TV and how they'd kissed on the floor after.

You look like Audrey Hepburn, he said.

Yeah, right, she said. Fat chance.

Don't, he said as he handed her more photographs.

There seemed to be over a hundred. She couldn't remember when or where they'd all been taken. In some of them she looked happier. Some she looked sad. In all of them she looked too fat, she thought.

And everyone at the exhibition saw these, she thought as she retreated into the couch.

She said to Derek, Someone should cut the photographs up and take the best feature, if there is one, and glue a figure out of them.

Derek stared at her.

You know, she explained. Look through a pile of eyes and noses and arms and legs and the rest. She gestured with a wave but then interrupted herself. Oh no, that's right. Too glossy. Not lightfast. It means I'd deteriorate over time. Isn't that a cool word, *lightfast*?

Diana and I started really talking when she saw these. She thinks you are too thin.

And did she show you pictures of any of her old boyfriends?

But before Derek could answer, Peggy-Leigh said, Oh, no, that's right, I forgot, she's in fashion, not photography. Maybe she had samples of their underwear for her portfolio?

Derek started to put the photos away. Why are you so angry? he asked softly, without meeting her eyes.

Why am I? she wondered.

This is a hangover talking, she said.

No, it isn't, he said looking up.

I'm angry because I feel like a sea monkey, Peggy-Leigh said, on the verge of tears again.

Shit, I cry a lot, she thought.

Derek came and sat beside her on the couch. He put his arm around the blanket.

She felt like a big jelly-roll. Everything is always about food, isn't it? she asked herself. But she let herself lean into Derek. Too hell with Diana, she decided.

A sea monkey? I don't understand he said kissing her hair, or where her hair would have been.

In those photos I look like a sea monkey, you know, those ads at the back of the comics I used to read at the cabin. You sent away for these sea monkeys who weren't alive until you put them in a fish bowl of water and then they were supposed to smile and wave and be yours.

Derek kissed her ear.

Well, she went on, it never happened. I added water and they stayed like tiny twigs. Nothing happened. Maybe I got a bad batch, but I thought it wasn't fair. And I thought it was me, I'd done something wrong again.

He kissed her on the mouth. She turned her face and opened her mouth, God, she'd missed him.

You're not a sea monkey, he said undoing the blanket. You're beautiful.

He began to lift her sweater.

She remembered lifting the same sweater over her head just a few days before at the hospital. They wanted to take photographs of her in her underwear.

For your record, the woman said.

I have a record? thought Peggy-Leigh. Attempted murder, she thought it must be. I'm just trying to kill the fat, not the rest, she wanted to tell them but didn't.

I don't think I can do that, she'd said to the nurse or doctor in white.

The white was too bright, it made her squint. When she squinted, the woman squinted. Maybe she thinks this is how I communicate, Peggy-Leigh thought.

It would really help us if you could.

The two of them looked at each other in the small room.

Just down to your bra and panties.

The words made her shiver.

Only a second, said the woman who must have seen her shiver and thought she was cold.

Peggy-Leigh wanted to cooperate. She wasn't sure why she did, but she did. And anyway, the doctors there would see she was really not anorexic or anything and they'd tell her not to bother coming back again, she was sure.

Okay, she said glad she'd worn a bra for once.

Then in her head she said, pretend you are not here, pretend this is happening to someone else. Picture yourself outside this big grey building. Picture yourself walking away. Walking past the art college down the street. Why not go in? Why not stand in front of the large colourful works she could see through the glass walls? Rest in a ceilingless space.

They'd given her a copy of the photo. She didn't want one, didn't want to look but didn't want to be difficult.

Thank you, she said, as if she'd just posed for Sears Portrait Studios. She wouldn't put this one on a Christmas card.

When the white woman left her to get dressed, Peggy-Leigh looked at the photo. And she cried. Because her thighs were too fat. And the top of her body was just ugly. But mostly because the young woman in the photo was looking down very sadly as if to say, This is all there is.

After the photo, the questionnaire had taken two hours and the white woman kept asking her if she was tired, if she could still read, if she could understand the questions.

This survey really helps us, she said, so it's important you fill it out as truthfully as possible. And if you're too tired, we can let you finish tomorrow.

Peggy-Leigh was pretty sure she was never coming back again so she thought she'd better finish it in one sitting.

Do you sometimes eat large quantities of food in a very short time? it asked.

She paused.

Which question? asked Our Lady of the Snows.

Peggy-Leigh liked her better when she thought of her as soft snow. This one, she said. And she read it to the woman.

Do you binge?

Peggy-Leigh frowned, she didn't know what that meant.

I think so, she said embarrassed.

It's okay, the woman said. What do you eat then?

Peggy-Leigh wanted to run now. This was getting too scary. She didn't say anything. The words were starting to blur and her fingers felt cold, she was afraid she would drop the pencil. Ice cream? asked the woman.

No.

Peggy-Leigh would have had to go down to the residence cafeteria at dinner time to get ice cream. All the girls were there then, she couldn't do that.

Chips, she said.

Okay, said the woman. How much?

A lot, said Peggy-Leigh.

It's okay, said the woman. It would help us if you tell us how much. Can you do that?

Peggy-Leigh shook her head.

We can help you, the woman said.

I don't think so, thought Peggy-Leigh. I want to go home.

The woman was waiting.

A bag, Peggy-Leigh finally whispered.

The woman looked at her. And then? she asked.

What?

What do you have after the bag and how big is the bag?

Peggy-Leigh started crying, This is too private, she told herself. Don't tell.

A small bag? The kind you get at the subway?

No, she choked, A big one, you know, family size.

Peggy-Leigh sighed. She was still alive, amazing.

Just one? said the woman like she didn't believe her.

Yes, she said thinking isn't that enough?

It was disgusting to Peggy-Leigh. She hated herself the four times she'd done it in the months she'd been at university.

That's not much, said the woman. You must mean more.

And so Peggy-Leigh thought, Even at this I am screwing up. I can't even binge right. I'm sorry, she said.

The woman studied her.

Fuck off, thought Peggy-Leigh, Leave me alone.

Derek was easing her sweater over her head. It caught on some of the earrings and Peggy-Leigh had to help unhook it.

He stared at her a long moment.

It's the men's undershirt, she thought. He hates it.

You look sexy, he said.

That made her smile. She almost laughed. She'd started wearing undershirts because she was always cold. They were soft and made her feel she was about six years old.

Here, said Derek. He was taking the quilt away from her.

He spread it on the floor, and pushed the milk-crate coffee table out of the way.

Don't move, he said. I'll get us my blanket.

Peggy-Leigh took the opportunity to untie her bandanna belt and to step out of her skirt. She stayed in her undershirt and white slip, but she took her black tights off. She was pleased by how relaxed she still felt.

Must be Ted, she thought. He's taught me lots.

Derek returned with the grey blanket he'd had on his bed at home.

She was glad to see it but found herself imagining colours to add to the grey – some blue, some green, a little watercolour and some benzine. Derek stretched out beside her on the quilt on the floor and covered them up with the blanket. He'd brought two pillows too. Peggy-Leigh didn't want to think one was Diana's.

She said, Do you sleep with her?

And she also said, Take off your clothes.

Derek looked at her. Take off your slip, he said as he began unzipping his jeans.

And then they were naked, almost, beneath the blanket. She couldn't take off her panties, because Ted had always done that. She hoped Derek would. He did. And soon they both cried out even though they'd done things other than intercourse.

I'm not ready for that, Peggy-Leigh had said.

Derek had seemed quite content with what she was ready for.

I love you, he said after.

She looked at the lights in the high-rise across the way. The living-room window had no curtains. Peggy-Leigh was glad they weren't in Derek's bed or Diana's. Maybe they only had one bed, she didn't want to know. She was warm and snuggled up against Derek. And for once she didn't feel hungry.

Do you love me? he said.

Sure, she said thinking of Diana.

Talk to me, he said. What are you thinking.

I like this, she said.

I do too, he said.

I mean sex, she said.

Derek stopped moving his hand up and down her left arm. He rolled away from her. She had to turn to look at his face.

What about us?

What *about* us? she asked.

Aren't we back together? he finally said.

She thought then about how his hip bone had hurt her. He *had* lost weight, she was right about that. While they were kissing they kept talking, trying to catch up. She asked him why he was bony and he'd said he didn't drink as much beer any more, he couldn't afford it, he said. One week all he'd eaten was popcorn. His student loan was fucked up he said, and they weren't processing it so he was broke. He ate popcorn and smoked. He said he was now up to a pack a day, the course was that stressful and he was that busy.

Why hadn't Diana helped him out? she asked.

We're not like that, he said.

And before she could know any more, and she wasn't sure she wanted to, he said, We keep our finances separate. Her parents are splitting up over money.

So they *are* sleeping together, she thought. And she concentrated on what Ted looked like. What his mouth felt like, what his hands did. Later, the next day and for the next weeks, Peggy-Leigh counted how many shadowy figures had been under the blanket with the two of them. At least two more people were there – Ted and Diana, maybe she should introduce them to each other, she thought, and then quickly dismissed the idea. She didn't want to give up Ted. She didn't want to give up Derek either, and she'd told him that, but she'd also told him, There is no us.

How can you say that? he said sounding frustrated.

This is exactly what I want to avoid, she thought. She looked at the vines on her skirt. They had tied up a chair.

We're too young, was all she said.

Who else are you seeing? he asked sitting up.

Someone, she said. And don't cry again, she said, I can't take it.

You can't take it! he said grabbing his jeans. How the fuck do you think I feel! Boy, he said standing up and doing up his zipper, you are one messed-up woman.

He shook his head and Peggy-Leigh knew he was crying.

She was too.

Dammit, she said. Go to hell, she told herself.

But Derek thought she was saying it to him.

Stay here tonight, he said leaving for his room. But I don't think I can see you any more. I can't watch you kill yourself, he said.

Where did that come from? she asked the lights outside the house as they leaned in. I'm not killing anybody, she told herself.

And she felt her hip. It was sharper, the feel of it soothed her. It had hurt when it hit Derek's when there was all that passion stuff. And the sound. It had made them both stop and look at each other.

The sound, there in the living room, seemed to echo. It reminded Peggy-Leigh of the culvert in Willow Junction. When she was a kid they weren't supposed to go near it. The big metal tube had been put under the street. The creek flowed through it and you could enter the tunnel from either side. She used to walk through it, they all did. You spread your legs and arms so that you were like a star. The water, which was only about a foot deep, if that, streamed between where your feet walked the sides of the tunnel. Your hands pressed the inside of the tunnel beside your head. You could stand straight up if you weren't too tall and as you grew you bowed your head as if praying. It was bad to fall in the water, even if it wasn't deep enough to drown, so you inched your way from one end of the greyness to the other by moving the points of your star, one at a time.

The meeting of Derek's hip with hers had made her think of the tunnel and how in the middle you thought you were never going to get out.

The Bubble Star

•

As she silently chanted *Ontario Northland*, since the words were on a pamphlet tucked into the back of the seat in front of her, she wondered if she should be looking into it. She'd read all the literature for years. How could she avoid it, breast cancer articles were everywhere. All the magazines talked about it, so did the newspaper. The radio and TV talked about one in ten. Then one in nine. She had stopped listening then, or tried to.

Peggy-Leigh had been afraid of it for as long as she could remember practically. She couldn't say she'd always been afraid of breast cancer, that would be lying. She could remember wanting her breasts to be bigger when she was in grade eight and still didn't wear a bra because she couldn't, nothing was that small. What was she supposed to do in gym class? Wear an undershirt?

And then her breasts had started growing. It was always a love-hate relationship she had with them. Then they were too big, boys were staring. They made her feel clumsy. What was she to do with them on dates?

This is why I had the dream, she thought on the train as it sat in Union Station, still boarding. I have not made peace with you.

Piece, she thought.

A piece of her breast. Last night, in her sleep, a small piece was suddenly different.

It was a lump.

She folded her arms across her chest to see if she could feel it. Her winter jacket was too thick, she couldn't feel any small hardness which she imagined as a planet. It spun in the solar system that was her breast. Her left one. It had always been smaller by a fraction, magazines she read as a teenager said that was normal. Normal but not nice.

Just weeks ago she'd thought her bra fit better on that side. Maybe they were making bras better. She had become aware of the money that was suddenly in the industry, there were huge billboards near their downtown home – women stretched out in their underwear. Black. Snowflakes stood out against the lace. Or there was the woman in white who was lit so brightly she looked like the moon if you didn't focus or were in a car driving too fast. There seemed to be several moons then in the Toronto night. What did her husband think of these billboards so close to their townhouse? She didn't know.

What did he think of the companion she had, the small dreamed-of dot close to her heart? She didn't know. She hadn't told him. He would react, want her to go see their doctor right away. He would want to fix her fear. That would mean fast action and she wasn't ready for any of that.

I can't rush this one, she thought, meaning her art. When I do, they are awful and just feel messed.

But why breast cancer was now tied to her latest mixed media work, she didn't know. I must have been reading too much, she guessed.

The snow had begun to lightly descend. The compartment she was sitting in was half in the station and half out. Her seat was exactly where outside met inside, and the snow fell in front of her. Her back was beyond the snow line. It made her think of the collage of her that Cynthia had done years ago, and had insisted she keep.

Called *Heads or Tails Peggy-Leigh*, it was of two female bodies in profile made from black fabric. A pair of Peggy-Leigh's black jeans to be exact, which had become way too big. One body was fat. One was skinny. They were facing each other. Cynthia and Peggy-Leigh had received top marks for that one, the instructor having missed or not cared about the bubbles on the back of the canvas which the roommates had had to fill with glue shot from a hypodermic needle they'd conned out of a not-very-bright dentistry student named Eddie. The collage had been large and heavy, and the canvas had had to be taken off Cynthia's easel and put on the floor so they could press hard enough. The pockets on the back of the collage, which had made Cynthia shriek at first, were not a disaster, assured Peggy-Leigh as she unloaded the needle and said, Open wide.

Peggy-Leigh traced the downward path of one big flake. She

didn't care if anyone was watching her draw her gloved hand down the glass. She hoped she was sitting the right way – she couldn't ride backwards, it made her dizzy. Like eating mint leaves.

Imogene could eat mint leaves. Once, when they were kids, she'd found a soft clump of them on their grandmother's property, up in the rocks.

Try this, she said holding a green fist of leaves out to Peggy-Leigh.

Yeah, right, she said. It's poison ivy, isn't it?

Imogene made a face, Would I be holding it if it was?

Good point, thought Peggy-Leigh. She didn't say this.

She stuck a waxy leaf in her mouth. Wintergreen, like mints her grandmother always had in her purse. She never left home without her tin of pink mints. She offered them during car trips while telling Iris, her daughter, Keep it between the ditches, okay?

The mints made Peggy-Leigh dizzy but she didn't want to hurt her grandmother's feelings. She'd take one, and then put it in the backseat ash tray she was sitting beside. There were a lot of mints in there sometimes, the lid would not close, but the car always smelled nice.

Wintergreen, said Peggy-Leigh. I think I'm allergic. She spat the leaf out.

Oh, said Imogene. Too bad.

The whole episode reminded Peggy-Leigh of a photo of the two of them on the road at the cabin. She was trying to feed a raspberry to Imogene who was in a stroller. Fat hands reached for the berry. It was a lovely captured moment and Peggy-Leigh could see why her mother and her grandmother both had framed it with gold frames from Towers, but it was the moment that had come just before that Peggy-Leigh really remembered.

Her father and mother had charged at her, thinking Peggy-Leigh was about to poison her little sister with deadly nightshade or a red roadside berry that would kill on contact. Both parents had yelled and lunged. Peggy-Leigh, who was four, had cried, afraid of the commotion.

Commotion was her mother's word.

After giving the all-clear, her parents started praising her for the fine raspberry and saying wasn't she sweet to be giving her little sister such a perfect berry. Peggy-Leigh offered the leaking fruit. Her fingers had berry juice on them and it made her think of blood. The whole incident had shaken her.

My first lesson in how actions can be misinterpreted, thought Peggy-Leigh as the train made its first moves.

I wonder, how will they take my coming home? Peggy-Leigh asked the window as she took off her gloves.

Will they think I've left him? Or he has left me?

Ted, she thought. I need to do this.

In their eight years of marriage, he had been nothing but devoted. She couldn't say the same. But she'd never acted on her traitorous thoughts. Not really.

Peggy-Leigh realized she probably needed to do a lot of things. And the trip back to Bay Lake and then Willow Junction was the big part of the whole. The train only stopped in Bay Lake. Her father would pick her up. Then they would drive the short drive home.

The story she was sticking to, about why she was visiting now, was that she needed to do research for her latest collages. And she had a grant to back her up. Her family seemed to be more accepting of her art when she could say it was government-funded. Or when she had a showing. They said they weren't sure they got it, but they were proud of her.

Whatever that means, she'd say to herself, shaking her head the way she used to when she was little and there was lake water squishing around.

The collages involved the quintuplets who were born near Bay Lake and Willow Junction. There was a museum there. And the doctor's house was open for viewing. In her mind she could already see the sign for the museum – five girls in black outline, shadows they looked like, on a white background.

Another sign had their heads in profile, and this sign used to scare Peggy-Leigh when she was a girl. It was as if the five had been beheaded.

Maybe I've read too much British royal history, too many wives, too much Lady Jane Grey.

She read a lot. Always had. When she was little, she was allowed to tell her younger sisters to stop bugging her if she was reading, her mother had said. Playing didn't count. Watching TV was just asking for it. But reading was off limits.

Imagine having four sisters, she said to herself as the train man looked at her ticket. She was glad no one was sitting opposite her for the five-hour ride. No one was looking at her all that time and staring at the bead inside her breast. Just a dream, she told herself as she crossed her arms again. Then she uncrossed them realizing she would roast in her sheepskin jacket. The train was always overheated. Or not-heated. It was one extreme or the other. She could remember trips back and forth from the campus to home when she was a student. The heat totally went off in January, just after the Christmas break, two years in a row. She had done up her coat then, worn her scarf, hat, and two pairs of mitts. But she was very thin then and couldn't seem to generate heat at the best of times.

It was the best of times, it was the worst of times, she thought to herself as the train left Toronto and the big snowflakes became even bigger. She wondered how close she had come. Some anorexics died, her therapist told her, trying to frighten her, she thought then. Now she guessed he was just being factual, respecting her intelligence and hoping that would save her. Maybe it had. She didn't know what had worked. Dr Baker surely deserved some credit, she thought, five years was a long time for him to listen to her or to listen to her silences.

Sometimes for fifty minutes she would not say anything. It wasn't that she didn't want to, and he seemed to sense that. She could tell he was just looking at her as she sat across from him and stared at the carpeting or his nice leather shoes. He always wore good socks.

Peggy-Leigh wasn't sure what the collages would be about. In lighter moments, she'd imagined stealing items from the quints' museum – a tiny shoe, a frilly white dress, a small piece of the oven door where the babies had been kept warm. Her grant application had said something about mixed media. Ted always helped her with application forms. And sometimes, in the end, the project resembled the proposal. Sometimes her art had a will of its own and she was merely the person who glued. Who affixed. Who looked at the puzzle pieces and then became an Ouija board, moving slowly and without strings.

The top floor of their townhouse, a kind of attic studio, was crammed with sketches, masonite, paper, paint, tubs of brushes left too long in water so that the room smelled sweet and cheesy. And if Peggy-Leigh reopened paints she'd added water to some time earlier, the smell in the studio was even stinkier, and the paint looked like grease.

Sometimes the smells were so bad she would open the window as wide as it would go and would swear off paint once more and use only fruit and vegetable juices for her wash. This would only last about a week. After that, she would work on the surface with paint, coloured chalk, and pencil crayons. Whatever was nearby was used, even ink, though she knew it was not as permanent. And neither were some lovely turquoisey and magenta tones she'd found recently, but she couldn't give them up.

Peggy-Leigh liked to layer her collages with very thin washes of colour, mostly acrylic, which she laid on like it was watercolour so that there was a kind of transparency. Sometimes before it was dry, she'd grab a sponge and rub back some of the paint. The paint collected in the textured spots produced an antique look which she liked, especially for collages about the quints. She hoped to use torn-up old newspaper clippings her grandmother had collected too. And she'd found some old postcards locked away in plastic food containers – the same way her grandmother stored buttons, twist ties, keys, nails, screws, and elastics. Peggy-Leigh figured that these images of the five girls could be combined with feathers, dried petals, grasses, and insect wings. She would fix them on top of a piece of a map that showed the old highway between Toronto and the quints' home, the road that millions had driven.

Scrapers for pressing were in her tool box, or were supposed to be there, as were some cheap brushes and small knives. There were shelves and shelves of paints in jars and tubes, yogurt containers, tins of chalk pastels, watercolours in pans, and ugly-looking sponges that stank. The only things that Peggy-Leigh seemed to be able to organize, really, were her caches of wallpaper strips, fabric slashes, and pages torn out of the million magazines that Ted teasingly said she kept in business.

She kept these materials in the two old waist-high filing cabinets, which acted as table legs for the door that acted as one of two tables. The filing cabinets she'd been given by her mother who said she could no longer manage without proper bookshelves for the cottage – Iris had said she was tired of pulling out books and magazines and wanted them to be displayed like in normal cottages. The door had been stolen from the cabin also, after lying on its side beside a bed and against a wall Peggy-Leigh's whole life. It had been in a house her father had lived in as a boy. He'd liked the wood and the plainness of it and had asked to keep it when his father had renovated and added something new and fancy to increase the resale price. Peggy-Leigh kept the doorknobs in a bowl on the windowsill.

The other table was a very basic but well-sized one that Ted had taken from one of the university hallways. No one ever used it for anything, he said, one evening after a function when Peggy-Leigh had remarked on how perfectly it would serve in her room. They had borrowed a maintenance truck to get it home.

There was only one bead in the dream. Waking in the middle of the night, she'd felt her breast as Ted lightly snored beside her. She had tried to imagine the small globe was blue, translucent glass, something beautiful. But in the stillness it had turned into something terrifying, like a crystal ball from childhood stories which could tell you the future, good or bad. Did she have a future?

She told herself of course she did. She had to focus on the new collage, go forward, add one piece on top of the others. On the train she would try not to feel for the bead. People wouldn't understand why a woman was pressing and poking her breast in public. Wouldn't understand she needed to know there wasn't a string of black pearls.

Even though it was afternoon, some houses had their Christmas lights plugged in. The grey snowy light made the lights brighter than a sunny day would have. Peggy-Leigh snuggled back into her seat and used her jacket as a pillow. She thought of beads.

Beads which had fallen off the back of a speeding truck as it rounded the corner on two wheels.

They'd been eating dinner at the cabin when the truck passed going way too fast. Then there'd been a sound they didn't recognize and the three girls had left the table to investigate. They'd mostly finished eating anyway. They were having oatmeal and toast for dinner. Sometimes they did that when their father wouldn't be there. The four of them liked this secret ritual. The man in their lives would never have gone for it.

The truck had lost at least part of its load. Peggy-Leigh found the first clear tube of beads among the rocks at the side of the dirt road. They were navy and had sparkles in them. Janis found a paint brush, a reed-thin one. Imogene had found the India ink. Jars of it, near the water's edge.

Probably some stuff fell in the lake, said Imogene.

All three girls looked into the calm water. They thought they could see things.

They were all thinking the same thing.

Not tonight, said Peggy-Leigh. He might come back and be angry. And besides, we just ate and have to wait an hour and by then it will be dark.

Right, said Imogene. After breakfast, after our hour, we'll bring our fins and masks.

Is it deep? asked Janis.

I'll help you, said Peggy-Leigh. It'll be just like we play underwater at our beach, only this time the treasure is real.

That summer they kept finding things. Sometimes when they walked by on the way to the point, the girls found more tubes of beads among plants at the roadside. Some of the brown India ink bottles matched the dried pine needles and so had been invisible at first glance. Twice they found rolls of what their mother said was rice paper.

It's used by artists, she said. I read about it.

So then the girls had played artist for days. It didn't matter that the paper was stained yellow from getting rained on and then drying out. If they'd found it right away, that night, it would have been snow-white, said their mother.

Peggy-Leigh thought there was regret in her mother's voice. And at first the girls were told not to use the stuff, surely the artist would come back for the beads and ink and brushes. No one showed up at their cabin to claim the loot. After a while it became routine for the girls to bring back another find. Maybe this is why I dreamed I have something in my breast, thought Peggy-Leigh as the train passed hydro poles. It's because I stole long ago.

Maybe I should have told someone about finding the beads.

She recognized the glass insulators were bead-like in their colouring – green, turquoise, and deep blue on top of the poles. The wires ran through the glass, a dark string.

Peggy-Leigh figured it was a good thing the insulators were up as high as they were. Otherwise people would have stolen them for their great colours. The lighter ones reminded her of baby colours, the tranquil shades of infants' clothing and stuffed animals. She liked all that stuff, always had, but she'd noticed in the last year she'd felt sad when she came upon it all in a gift shop. Something would give way inside her. Like a trap door. She'd feel confused then, there in a store as a sales person inevitably said, Can I help you?

I wish you could, Peggy-Leigh would say and that would usually get rid of the clerk, at least temporarily.

Who can help me? she'd ask herself, leaving the store.

Lately, when this strong moment would hit her, she'd think, what is the trap? If this is the door, which way am I going? Is wanting to have kids a trap?

Would she feel trapped then? At home with a child while Ted disappeared every day to give his lectures at the university? What about her art?

Somedays she could imagine continuing with her collages, baby strapped on board her body, non-toxic glue on her fingers. But could she count on harnessing the baby for say, the first seven years? Until the child could be safely semi-independently on its own in the house and at school?

Peggy-Leigh didn't think you could expect a child to be quiet until it was, say, over five and could play on its own. But didn't some women breast-feed until the child was three? Hadn't she heard of stories where the mother was still breast-feeding the kid when it was six?

Peggy-Leigh shuddered. It was the word breast that had done it. Go back to the baby thing, she told herself and chanted *Baby, Baby, Baby,* in time to the train on the tracks.

She didn't know what the trap was, she just knew there was one and maybe she was already in it. She was so sure when she married Ted that she didn't want kids. He was sure too. Even though he'd already been married four times, by the age of forty-five, he didn't have any kids. So she was nobody's stepmother. She was somebody's fifth wife.

It amazed her. She felt like one of the Gabors, was it Zsa Zsa? How many times was the real Peggy Lee married? she asked her mother, Iris.

Iris didn't know and didn't know that her eldest daughter had married a man who'd already said, I do, more than once before. Peggy-Leigh's standard line was that Ted had an ex-wife. He did. And another. And another, and another. There were explanations for all of them, which Peggy-Leigh accepted from the beginning.

She watched a town go by. She was glad she didn't live there. It looked small and quiet with few distractions and everyone would know everyone and she would have to explain the four ex-wives if she lived in a place like that.

Immigration, she would say.

Pregnancy-scare, another one had a mother who was dying and her father had been murdered, no kidding, and the last had been to please the bride's religious parents.

All plausible. And Ted was such a warm, caring soul, to a fault she sometimes thought, that she could see what had moved him to marriage. She didn't want to think about why he'd wanted to marry her. Didn't want to add *eating disorder* to the list. And besides, she was over that now, had been for years, had been a recovering anorexic for just about a decade, and Ted hadn't left her. In fact, he seemed to love her as much as that first night long ago, when he'd asked her in for tea. When he'd taught her things. When he'd lied to her when she'd asked, Are you married?

He was, it turned out, to wife four. But they were separated. If you could call it that. She was away for a week visiting her religious parents. She'd called it a retreat as she'd left him, apparently.

When Ted had finally told Peggy-Leigh, months later, when she'd asked why they never went to his house any more, he'd said he never should have married his wife, but had, after two years of living together, only so that her parents who lived on the east coast would come and visit them. And that after the visit, Coralee, that was her name, had started talking about how they had too many possessions and how they should go to church. And how she didn't want to have sex any more because she felt she should only sleep with Jesus.

Jesus, Ted said he had said.

Coralee had looked at him and made the sign of the cross.

Jesus is dead for Christ's sake, Ted said.

I know, said Coralee. So you *do* understand, she went on, I knew you would.

And then she'd gone home and near the end of the week Ted had called Peggy-Leigh for pizza, she was pretty sure that's how it had gone.

But she didn't focus too much on the details back then. She was just trying to get through university. To switch her major to Fine Arts, realizing it was her only way of passing since it was the only thing she worked on. Was just trying to get through lunch. And dinner. All the rest. Through psychiatric appointments and meetings with dietitians. Daily weigh-ins. A couple of hospitalizations when tubes ate for her. She'd stare at the pipes running into herself and she'd say, How's lunch? Would you like some fries with that? She had to keep her sense of humour, and her family's. They would stare at the tubes and her bones and would lose their ability to talk. They would look back at her with fish faces, and mouths that opened and closed without words. Peggy-Leigh wished they were orange, with bulging eyes. Or red and blue, like the fighting fish she and her father once bought who killed each other in a plastic bag on the drive home.

Must be why they had them in separate tanks in the store, said her father, trying to explain. And why they gave us two bags for them. They could have told us, eh, sweetie?

Japanese fighting fish, Imogene said later to Peggy-Leigh. What were you thinking?

Peggy-Leigh and her father bought angel fish after that. And goldfish, which were orange and so should have been renamed, thought Peggy-Leigh. And the aquarium was fairly stable after that, once they got the expensive pump and filter system and siphon and all the paraphernalia as her mother called it with her back to them when they arrived home each time from the pet store. Peggy-Leigh and her father cleaned the green slime from the sides of the tank a lot and then bought an ugly fish that ate it all. The cat watched the fish. Sometimes he slept on the lid of the tank while Peggy-Leigh slept in her bed. In the morning the fish looked exhausted, she thought, like they'd been awake all night waiting for the end.

The end came during a thunderstorm. One morning Peggy-Leigh was lying in her bed and was looking at her window and wishing she had closed it in the night, but it had been humid.

Peggy-Leigh knew about lightning. There was the big fire up the road from the cabin. And a tree limb was struck years later and it fell on the cabin and dented the roof right above the bed Peggy-Leigh thought she could have been killed in.

And one time her grandmother's clock above the sink was hit. As was a great-aunt whose name escaped her, who was standing between an open door and an open window one summer afternoon on the prairies. Peggy-Leigh couldn't remember if the aunt had died. She didn't think so. She thought she just set off airport alarms, couldn't wear those new digital watches, and made batteries die.

Peggy-Leigh was thinking all this and was hoping Imogene would come into her room, thinking she could wake up her older sister since their father would already be at work and their mother was in Toronto with their grandmother to see a specialist for something or other.

And then a flash in through the screen, over her bed, right to the metal top of the fishtank where the lights had been left on all night. A cracking sound. Sharp and final.

Peggy-Leigh hit the floor and was shaking. In her pyjamas she slid along the floor, up the wall, and looked out the window. Men who were digging the ditch at the end of her driveway looked back at her.

Everything okay in there? one called.

Peggy-Leigh didn't know what to say. I think so, she finally managed.

That confirmed it, something had happened. She closed her window. Then she hit the floor again and slithered out of her room, along the carpet in the hall, to her sister's room.

Imogene had not been impressed. As Peggy-Leigh shook her sister's sleeping shoulders, Imogene said, Cut it out, Benny.

Peggy-Leigh kept poking her sister and said, close to hysterics, Wake up! My fish were hit!

You don't have fish, Benny, said Imogene rolling over.

I'm not Benny, dammit.

As it usually did for her father, swearing seemed to get through, and Peggy-Leigh allowed herself to slump down on her bum on Imogene's bedroom floor.

What are you doing here? asked Imogene.

My fish were struck by lightning, I could have been killed.

Sure. Look, if you want me up just say so. What time is it?

Really, said Peggy-Leigh pleading. C'mon, I'll show you.

And then realizing she was the older sister and as such was expected to be in charge when their parents were out said, Come with me, in what she hoped was a strong voice.

As they walked down the hall they heard cartoon noises from the family room. Janis must have been up.

Well, at least the TV wasn't hit, said Peggy-Leigh trying to sound in control.

I think you're nuts, said Imogene, they better have been hit.

What they saw made the two sisters stop. Stop talking, stop moving, stop fighting.

One by one the goldfish slowly stopped swimming, lost their balance, and drifted upside down up toward the aquarium lid light. The light which wasn't on now. The light which as usual had stayed on all night so that if she woke up, Peggy-Leigh could lie in bed, under her Barbie comforter, which she knew she really should have given up, watching her fish swim between the green stems.

The light must have blown out, said Peggy-Leigh finally.

Sorry, said Imogene.

Dad can get me a new bulb.

No, I mean about your fish. It looks like they're all going to die.

Peggy-Leigh was afraid she was going to cry. Not all of them, she managed to say without looking at her sister. Do you think?

Imogene put her hand on the glass tank. It's warm, she said. Should you unplug the stuff?

Peggy-Leigh didn't know. Nothing was working. Not the light, not the pump – there was no soothing hum – and the filters didn't have any bubbles streaming from them. She figured she might as well disconnect it all.

Stop life-support, she said.

All the fish *had* died by the time their father got home from work. And the light never really worked on one side again. The side that hadn't been hit worked but after two new bulbs Peggy-Leigh and her father gave up on full lighting.

Maybe I'm getting too old for fish, anyway, she thought as she sat on her bed. She traced Barbie's hair. And I should get rid of this, she thought. Maybe Janis will want it, Imogene won't.

Peggy-Leigh watched people getting ready for their stop. The woman down a ways had had her coat on for thirty minutes and Peggy-Leigh was sure the train was still ten minutes away from Huntsville.

Must want to be home, she said to herself. Do I?

Now there is a hard question, thought Peggy-Leigh. And why is it so hard? Don't I like them?

Of course she liked them, she decided, it wasn't like her family wasn't close. Maybe they were too close, maybe that was it. Everybody knew everything about each other. Like when Janis had called to tell her that Imogene was carrying Benny's baby. Five minutes later Iris called.

Can't talk right now, she said almost whispering, but your sister is pregnant.

If Janis hadn't just called, thought Peggy-Leigh as she said goodbye to her mother, I might not know which sister.

Peggy-Leigh had called Imogene right away to say she was

delighted. And, to her own mild surprise, she thought, I really am. Until then children were like a scene from the train Peggy-Leigh strained to make out. Was that a cow? No, it would turn out to be a rock. Or a tree stump. Was that a man in the woods? Sometimes it was a man in the woods.

Imogene will be terrific as a mother. And finally, maybe she and Benny can simplify things a bit and be together, thought Peggy-Leigh, though she didn't know how the logistics would work. She'll leave Russ. Or is it the other way around?

For the first time Peggy-Leigh saw her brother-in-law in a new light. Maybe he'd been trying to leave Imogene ever since he married her. Maybe he knew enough not to get close to her, ever, because maybe even he recognized the Benny factor.

The benefactor? Peggy-Leigh laughed out loud.

The woman with her coat on stared at her.

She's too hot, that's all, thought Peggy-Leigh, feeling good from the laugh. Undo your coat, she wanted to say. Loosen up, lady.

Good advice for me, she thought.

It's not cancer.

That was the first time she'd said the word, even in her head. There, she said, now I'm more in control.

The insulators going by were clear now, all of them. Colourless. You could see evergreens through them. Or sky that was turning from late afternoon to night the way it did in winter. No stages, just bang bang. No gradual shift of light.

Peggy-Leigh liked afternoon light the best. And it was funny, morning light was better for her collage work. Her top-floor studio was bright then, she didn't have to hold pieces of wallpaper under her lamp to see if they were burgundy or blue. At about four o'clock there were shadows everywhere. The world seemed to slow down.

And that was often when Peggy-Leigh was deep in making textures with a bristle brush. Stippling or using it like a scrub brush –both produced a marvellous vibration Peggy-Leigh felt through her whole body. And the raspy scratching sound on the surface would drown out all other intrusions – school buses stopping, cars honking, children yelling to each other. Ted knew never to call late in the day because even if he talked into the answering machine, or called to Peggy-Leigh, she wouldn't hear.

Sometimes she would realize later that she'd been staring for most of an hour at her favourite brush after cleaning it off – a bird's wing in a leaf handle which was a Chinese calligrapher's brush – a brush she'd used to write words on a collage, anticipating how beautifully they might eventually run, depending on the ink or paint. Other times, she would be stopped by something like how an old reliable watercolour brush that she'd had forever suddenly couldn't hold a point any more and the hairs had split up the middle, forming two points.

And then she would have to try it out in its new state, sometimes starting a new collage in the process, since the one she'd been working on was almost dry, the gel once thick and white having turned almost clear. Another collage would be in its pin-up stage, as she called it. And anyway, even if it just meant getting out a new piece of paper and readying it on the table for the next day, Peggy-Leigh always liked to feel that she was starting something as the skies got dark.

It was also, she realized, when she was quite tired lately. It reminded her of when she used to swim in the lake with Imogene. The two of them would battle the wind, swimming fearlessly against it, every now and then turning to wave to Janis and their mother on shore so they wouldn't worry. Then Imogene would swim up to Peggy-Leigh and the two girls would hold onto each other and, while still doing a kind of treading-water move, they would float, letting the current carry them.

If we were shipwrecked, Imogene said once as they bobbed, we'd save each other.

I guess we would, thought Peggy-Leigh as the station lights stopped beside her window and a painted sign said Huntsville.

The lady with the coat said, Bye, as she passed Peggy-Leigh.

And then the woman added softly, I hope things go okay.

Peggy-Leigh didn't know what that was about. She pretended to look for something in her purse. Must be about Imogene and the baby, she told herself. Or maybe I'm exhausted and should try to nap.

* * *

She woke just as the train was bypassing Willow Junction and was closing in on Bay Lake. Peggy-Leigh's first thought was Ted. Why hadn't she told him about the lump dream? Why did she think she could do this alone? Why wasn't he here?

If there'd been a phone on the train, the way it seemed to her there were a zillion of them on planes, she'd have phoned immediately and said, Get here.

And he would have. She knew Ted was fastened to her. Sometimes she guiltily figured he was more committed to their marriage than she was, since it seemed she tempted fate constantly, if not in deed, in thought. What if she saw Derek? What if he was divorced, living in Toronto and she found him by accident? What if, when she went for her passport photo, after the last one had expired, he was the photographer?

Walking into the back of the photography studio, the girl who answered the phones leading the way, Peggy-Leigh would look up and Derek would say, You?

The phone girl would look once and then dash out, pretending the phone was ringing.

Me, Peggy-Leigh would say.

And then he would say how he'd always loved her, how she was the reason it hadn't worked with Diana, and how he'd been too embarrassed to try to find Peggy-Leigh after the divorce because he could only land jobs at portrait studios where his clients were paying him to go to their cottages to take that informal shot where the sweaters all complemented each other, the hairdos were flawless, and the dog had just been blow-dried.

She used to have these thoughts a lot. She used to wonder what her relationships, not just sexual ones, all of them, would have been like if she'd been eating. If her electrolytes hadn't been considering a heart attack. If she had been able to remember the plot of the movie she'd gone to with Derek or someone else, three hours later. Things she thought about lately scared her in ways they hadn't scared her at the time.

And what if she hadn't found someone like Ted?

More like, she corrected her head, what if he hadn't found me? He saved my life.

She knew feminists wouldn't like it, sometimes even she wasn't sure she liked it. Didn't that give him a hell of a lot of power?

Who cares, she'd tell herself sometimes in her studio as she was collaging houses. Rooms. Sometimes just windows. Reaching for another jar, she'd read out loud, Grumbacher, Hyplar Medium. And then she'd think, gloss or matte? And this would lead to make-up, which would lead her to photographs of models in Toronto fashion magazines, which would lead to Derek and she would say, Do you love him? meaning Ted.

Of course I do. With all my heart.

Oh?

Well, most of it.

Except for that pie-slice bit, which is Derek's?

Maybe.

Hi, sweetie, she imagined her father would say, hugging her and taking her suitcase. They would walk to the truck in silence, but a good silence.

Once inside, with the engine running and the defrost on, Ray would say, Ted called, he got your note, he'd like you to call.

Okay, Peggy-Leigh would say and she'd mean it.

Father and daughter wouldn't say any more about it, but both would know they weren't saying

Everything okay?

Well, not quite yet, but I think it will be.

Can I do anything?

No, but thanks.

Peggy-Leigh knew the non-communication thing with Ted wasn't about love, wasn't dangerous. A lump was dangerous. And maybe she was trying to protect Ted from fear, the way he'd taken care of her, if that's how you could describe it. She knew she took care of him too, knew that their relationship was two-sided, it was just that her scratches and dents were more apparent, more surface-like. It's my turn, she thought, while thinking of her father who would be driving to meet her to drive her home, to be strong for Ted.

And how to do this? She had no idea.

The sign with the five girls was coming up. Peggy-Leigh concentrated on it. What if Imogene had two? Or more? She laughed.

What's so funny? her father was bound to ask in the car.

Do you know about Imogene?

If I didn't, wouldn't you have to tell me now? he'd say.

Peggy-Leigh thought about this and decided she wouldn't need to say anything because her father would turn to her with a big smile and say, I'm happy for her and Benny. I wish they didn't have to wait the rest of the nine months.

Then he would say as they turned onto the side road, Your mother is thrilled too. All those hats and mitts she's knitted over the years for the premature babies at St. Mary's. She's wanted a grandchild forever.

He will realize this might hurt me, thought Peggy-Leigh, why else would he take my hand?

Don't you need that to turn with? she'd joke.

Yeah, I guess I do.

* * *

As the train knocked closer to her father, Peggy-Leigh felt really sleepy, like it would be so easy to doze, but she was too close, she thought, wasn't she? Why can't I stay awake?

And then Derek was there, in the gallery, the opening night of her quint show. She recognized the back of his head. Walking across the space, her heels knocking on the shiny hardwood floor, she noticed at last they were alone.

There are worse things than having four sisters, you know?

Derek smiled back. He said nothing but his face said, Go on.

I'm gonna tell you some stuff I've been thinking about lately, Derek. What's worse than having four sisters? Having none. I can't really think about not having Imogene and Janis. But you know? I have imagined this. Because of breasts.

Derek looked like he'd heard wrong. His head tilted sharply.

Yes, breasts. You remember mine? I know you do, because I remember parts of you too, most often your hands.

And here, Peggy-Leigh took one of Derek's hands and led him to a cushioned bench in the middle of the vast hardwood space. It reminded her of a sandbar. They sat down. People around them moved slowly from collage to collage. Sometimes they stepped closer to the work. Other times, they stepped away.

You see, I went back to Willow Junction and Bay Lake. I went back for a couple of reasons. I thought the main one was doing this big project involving the quintuplets, the five sisters. Research, you know. See the site, all that. But I think now I was really going back because of a lump in my breast.

Derek was staring.

The left one. And no, you wouldn't have felt a lump back then. It was a nightmare I had.

Derek reached for her hand.

So, while I was out for a walk with Imogene, we were walking down main street actually, to see how things hadn't changed, I asked her if she'd ever checked her breasts. She looked at me really funny and I thought she'd say there I go again worrying about nothing but then she said she had a lump last year.

She said her doctor freaked out and sent her to a specialist but she couldn't get in for six weeks and thought she was dying.

Derek squeezed her hand.

Why didn't you tell me? I asked her.

She didn't want to tell anyone. She didn't tell Russ. He was way up north anyway, so that was easy.

Did Mom know? I asked her.

Imogene said, Are you kidding?

Was it …? I couldn't say the word. And I know I looked at her breasts to see if they both were there and I know she caught me.

Derek moved closer on the bench.

No, they drained it, Imogene said. They tested and it turns out Iris had it done three times. And Janis examines hers every two weeks.

Peggy-Leigh gasped for air. The gallery owner, Carl, was walking by and shot her a look. The look said *Mingle*.

You'd think sisters as close as we are would talk about such things, wouldn't you? Peggy-Leigh said to Derek's hand. And why haven't I known my mom has had three biopsies?

Derek shook his head.

So then I was crying in front of the doughnut shop and Imogene didn't know what was going on and then she thought I had breast cancer and had been told I was a goner and that's why I'd come home.

Peggy-Leigh leaned over and picked up a catalogue which had landed on the floor.

Do you remember touching my breasts in your father's car? Remember, we'd be in the parking lot behind the theatre and it would be winter and your jeans would still be damp because you'd washed them too late and hadn't let them dry before putting them on for the movie and how they'd freeze in the cold.

Derek smiled.

When I dreamt the lump, middle of the night in bed, I thought of you. Can you believe it? Well, of course I thought of Ted, of course I would think of him, but I didn't count on thinking of you. Didn't count on seeing you either.

Carl cleared his throat somewhere behind Peggy-Leigh. She turned just in time to see him place a red dot on the collage called *Five and Dime*. A bright blue wash smudged with red was punctuated by five black lace little girls' faces in profile. Ten black lace hands, stretched as if to say STOP! were dotted around the canvas.

Imogene said you'd been back in Bay Lake for a while now.

Derek nodded and took the catalogue from Peggy-Leigh.

Divorced? Imogene said you've been single for at least a few years in fact, and your wife has the kids.

Derek looked down at the prices listed.

I didn't ask if her name was Diana. I always thought I would, you know? I thought I would want to know, would want to see what could happen with us then, now, but there you were, in The Java Junction, buying beans.

Carl leaned over to hiss, *Three thousand. Maybe if you were nice to more people here, there could be a few more?*

Peggy-Leigh waved him away. She put her hand over the description Derek seemed to be trying to focus on. It was the collage called *The Official Photographer.*

Imogene and I were in the mall to look at baby things, even though it's way early and she and Benny, yes Benny, won't have the kid for lots of months yet. Anyway, we were avoiding Goodmart, and she wanted a muffin, she thinks she needs to eat for the baby every two hours, and just before we walked in, I saw you.

Do you know how many times I've imagined this in the last decade?

I don't. I just know I thought about what might happen and never once did I imagine I would grab Imogene by the arm and say, Be a sport.

And I dragged her into the sporting goods store right beside the coffee place.

I never pictured Bay Lake going for that upscale kind of stuff, you know, mochaccino, café au lait. Maybe I never gave the place the benefit of the doubt, I don't know, but I did like it there this time and wondered why I stay away so long between visits. The way I wonder why I didn't go up to you. You looked same as always, same as now. And I missed something then. But it wasn't you. It was something like how I feel now that I'm away from Imogene again. She's pregnant with her first child, she's the first of us to have a kid. My parents, as you'd expect since you know them, are nuts with joy, and I'm not really there. I'm here in Toronto, and we talk almost every day on the phone, but there is this longing, this space where door and floor don't quite meet where the air cools in. The couples in front of three mostly green collages seemed suddenly to be talking louder. There was laughter. Peggy-Leigh wondered if the wine had started to kick in. That always made more sales. Carl insisted on an excellent selection and seemed to know just when to apologize and say that the wine had run out. He'd once explained to Peggy-Leigh that drunken patrons didn't buy, only tipsy ones.

Maybe I'm not making sense. I did miss you. I did miss something as I watched you hold a pound of beans and I wanted to know what kind they were and if you drink decaf or not.

But more, just then, with Imogene looking at me like I was nuts and why were we looking at hockey sticks, I missed Ted and the life we have together and I was so afraid my breast was going to kill us all and I'd deserve it because I tried to kill my breasts all those years I wouldn't eat or threw up or did laxatives. How could I have been so blind, I thought as I held a lovely new stick in my hands and read the name of a famous hockey player. His wife's breasts were implants, I knew that much. And just then it all seemed so ridiculous, I laughed and then in a rush I told Imogene all kinds of things. About you. And me. And not there, in the sports store, we went to a new restaurant that Janis told us to go to because we needed to see the bathroom she said. And for hours Imogene talked about Benny. And what it feels like to know you are pregnant.

And she was right.

And I am.

Pregnant, that is. And that's why I wanted to see you. Sort of. It's all connected somehow, but I don't know how, and I'm hoping you will. I don't have breast cancer. I just have bigger breasts. I'd stopped taking my birth control pill. I remember thinking about it, not actually forgetting to take it, and thinking quietly, I want Ted's child.

Derek gently moved Peggy-Leigh's hand away from the catalogue. He read the description of the photographer collage, looked slowly at the collages from where he sat, and stopped when he found it. For long moments, with his head turned from Peggy-Leigh, he gave away nothing.

I hope you can hear this. And I hope you want to hear this. All these years I've imagined you caring and wanting to know I was okay and I cannot believe you would have changed much from when we thought we loved each other. Or at least, you loved me. And I know now you knew what it was then, love, that is. I didn't have a clue. I think I might have done my best back then, but couldn't have loved you or me or Imogene or anyone.

And something else, my fear of sex? Or of what you wanted to do? Well, I know it wasn't just something you wanted to do for you, not totally, I mean, it's always about the person wanting something, but it's also about wanting something for the lover, isn't it?

Please don't think I'm crazy, or think these are just the hormones of a pregnant woman ranting. For once, I think I'm perfectly sane, whatever that means, and I'm happy. Whatever that means. Ted is wonderful, and I'm trusting that it won't hurt you to hear that. I wish you had someone. I used to think I wanted your relationship or marriage or whatever not to work out, because then maybe there would be a time when we'd get back together. But sometime ago, without my knowing, you sank back into the lake in my head and the man who surfaced was my husband who said, Let's swim to the island. And I did.

Derek seemed to have stopped listening. And then he stood up. Carl was approaching the two of them and Peggy-Leigh held her breath. She watched the two men talk briefly. Derek shook his head once. She thought she heard the word *shipped* but couldn't tell which man had spoken. And then Derek was nodding. Both men smiled and shook hands. Carl walked purposefully towards a collage, peeling off a red dot from his sheet as he did so. It was *The Official Photographer.*

Derek sat down on the bench again, this time leaving space between him and Peggy-Leigh.

So, Imogene's child will be older than mine, by quite a few months. And that's good. I'm not sure I'd want mine to be the oldest. I think Imogene and Benny's boy, or girl, will be more than capable and things somehow balance out this way.

Already this pregnancy has altered my world dramatically. You couldn't see anything, even if you looked really carefully right now, but this baby is as real as last night. Remember how much I used to dream? I still do, and still remember them vividly the next day and I tell Ted who can never remember anything about his. Last night's was good and bad. Kinda like life. There's no such thing as the perfect life, think about it, we have nothing to judge our lives against, there is no measure, is there? Anyway, the dream had water in it, as usual, only this time it wasn't the lake at the cabin, it was a pool.

Turquoise water smelling of chlorine. No one was swimming, the water was just rolling slightly on its own while I sat near the edge with my baby. I don't know if it was a boy or girl. The child was blond. Don't know how that happened. And my mother was there too. I really wanted to talk to her, needed for her to listen to me about something – I wish I knew what it was – but I knew she heard nothing, it was as if I was making no sounds, the words just diving under the water and staying there. I knew she was absorbed in her grandchild, couldn't help herself. And that she and I would never again communicate the way we once had.

I remember in the dream I felt sadness and happiness all at once and a longing for that combination to be okay. I tried to concentrate on the colour of the pool and my child's hands in the air and my mother's laugh and smile. I hadn't made that look on her face, that sound from her throat and beyond, and of course I was a mix then. Like water I was both wetness and air, and for the rest of my life I'm not the same in her life, my mother's, and she is different in mine and my child becomes stronger in both lives every second. The order has changed, someone shuffled the deck, there are face cards everywhere.

When I woke I thought, Everything is different. And yet everything that was, still hangs on. My baby is composed of every moment up until now, and now, and now.

Derek nodded slowly, a smile forming. He watched Peggy-Leigh wave back to a laughing woman who was pointing at a big yellow collage. Carl was heading for it.

I wouldn't put it past Janis to get pregnant too. When I was home she brought her friend Domino for us to check out. He's more than a delight, he's brilliant and lovely. And gay. And they told me, actually, Janis told me, and over the phone last week, that they were talking about having a child together. And for some reason I'm not surprised, or scared for them, and that probably *is* my hormones. But they are talking about AIDS testing and taking their time and she figures they'll talk about things for a year. Domino would be such a good dad. And Janis, well, she's the tender-heart she's always been compared to her sisters. If we were ever to be quints, it would have been best if there'd been five of her, I think.

Derek shook his head slightly. He stood up and reached for Peggy-Leigh's hand and pulled her to her feet.

I guess you're saying, That's all for now. It's so good to say these things at last to you, if only at an opening, and I hate in a way to let you go. I bet we'll meet in The Java Junction sometime when Ted and I are visiting Ray and Iris, and Imogene will be there trying to untangle two strollers.

Derek kissed her cheek, looked straight at her for a long minute and then seemed to motion her to walk with him to the exit. Peggy-Leigh kept talking.

And you'll buy me a coffee and you and Ted will do some sort of subtle checking out of each other. And I'll meet your wife.

Derek was still smiling and his hand turned the door handle as if to go. There were people standing behind them arguing loudly about one of the collages.

Wait, Peggy-Leigh said to Derek. He stepped back from the door in case anyone wanted in.

The other night I had to attend a dinner party. Ted gets us invited to a lot of these and, because he likes most of the other professors, we go. I'm used to it now. And even have a good time sometimes, like the other night. Aron and Celia are loving and funny. They have no kids, instead, their home is a warm gallery or funny museum. We enjoy going there, even if, at times, the talk is only about university stuff.

Aron got a new telescope. He's head of the astronomy department and he's so excited about his work all the time that it's hard to believe he gets paid for it. That's what he says.

Someday they will realize I would do all of this for free and then where will we be? he always asks.

Divorced, calls Celia from the kitchen.

This is not true, and anyway, she makes as much as he does. She runs an advertising company, which is how Aron learned of the new telescope. New technology. New price. Buyers needed, she had said, people with big disposable incomes or university budgets. Aron bought one for the department, and one for himself, and got the good two-for-one discount. I'm not sure it's ethical, but I like them so I don't care. And the machine, if that's what you call it, is a dream.

Derek led Peggy-Leigh to three steps, which went into Carl's office. He sat down on a step and patted beside him. Peggy-Leigh joined without pausing her story.

That night, near the pool, listening to the telescope hum as it repositioned itself, I realized how men are drawn to war. It's not the fighting, the thrill of battle, all that. It's the gear. The bells and whistles, as they used to say. It's the buttons, the computer beeps, the remote control.

I have to say, I liked the new telescope as much as the stars.

Is that bad? What does it say about me? I'm afraid of what you will think.

But I tell you this, because that hour or so, in the damp night that smelled of dirt, was the most real I've felt.

Aron had carried out the big machine while we were all drinking tea by the fireplace. It was cold enough for a fire. He then kept calling to us from outside – we thought he was clowning around – we had somehow missed his lugging of the equipment – anyway, I finally went to quiet him and as I stepped past the patio doors, the world opened out like a vat and I was sucked in.

Do you ever go to dinner parties? I wonder so much about you. Have you ever, like me that night, felt as if time was controlled by your breathing?

Derek seemed to want her to go on.

I'm doing a poor job of explaining what I learned. And I can't for the life of me say what it has to do with the moon, the stars, the formations of whatever technical term they are. It's just that as I was squinting into the lens, closing my left eye, I saw things.

Did you know you can wade on the moon?

I swear it looks like anyone could wade just the way you would through the water around Bay Lake, Willow Junction, anywhere we know. You can see indentations on the moon, which look like dents in a sandbar as you look at your feet through the water. I imagined you could drag your hand across the moon and leave lines there just as a rake would.

And then Aron talked of a bubble star.

Glancing back at the swimming pool light beneath the surface, I tasted the words in my mouth over and over. The cold air churned everything – chlorine and leaves and recently cut grass and the pond at the end of their property. I could hear the thick green water soaking the rock border and waving the reeds and rushes in the breeze when the wind grew stronger.

She was holding Derek's hand again, still on the steps.

That's when it hit. As I said, I don't know why, there's no apparent connection that I can see. But suddenly there it was, this thought I had, how men and women, or girls and boys, for that's really more like what people are at the time, shouldn't have to deal with sex at all until after they've been together a substantial time. Really. It was so clear to me then, looking up into the clear clear night sky. It's all about sex. And there's no way anyone should have to deal with that *before*.

The order's all mixed up, don't you think? It's like looking at the big dipper and having the stars out of order. The shape would be something else then, wouldn't it?

I worry you'll think I'm mad.

Worse, I worry you won't think of me at all.

I don't want to talk to you about sex. At least, not about sex as I understand it now having lived these years with Ted, and I'm sure you're relieved to hear this. And the bubble star, it turns out, was my hearing misleading me again. There is no bubble star, as beautiful as it may sound. There is, instead, the double star. A star made of two gravitationally bound stars. They revolve around a common centre of gravity.

And we, Derek, are the double star.

I don't mean specifically you and me. I mean men and women, male and female. At some point in any relationship, and this is what hit me that telescope night, the lovers become this double star. And you know what? This never happens on the first night, it can't, it takes years, you know?

I just think, from where I stand now, that we were ill-informed. And it's still going on. Sex is so much better *after*. After what? I don't know. Just after. Making love is like the waves on the moon billions of years later. Why didn't any of us know?

She reached for his other hand too and this made Derek completely face her.

I thought of you then as I stood that night on the lawn's wet grass. And this is what I wanted you to know. With my left eye closed, my face tilted into the lens of the telescope, I said in my head, Look, Derek.

•

Lesley-Anne Bourne was born in North Bay, Ontario, in 1964, and received an Honours B.A. from York University and an M.F.A. in Creative Writing from the University of British Columbia.

Three collections of her poetry have been published: *The Story of Pears* (1990), which was a finalist for the Gerald Lampert Award; *Skinny Girls* (1993); and *Field Day* (1996). She is the recipient of the Milton Acorn/Air Nova Poetry Award, the Banff Centre's Bliss Carman Award for poetry, and the Carl Sentner Fiction Award. In 1994 she was honoured with the Air Canada Award, administered by the Canadian Authors' Association, for a Canadian writer under thirty who shows outstanding promise. *The Bubble Star* is her first novel.

Lesley-Anne lives in Charlottetown and, since 1989, has taught at the University of Prince Edward Island.